REVELATION

RAYNA NOIRE

Published by Sleeping Dragon Press.
Copyright 2014, Rayna Noire

Revelation
ISBN-13: 978-0615982069
ISBN-10: 0615982069

Pagan Eyes
Revelation Book Two

CHAPTER ONE

His eyes sparkled with humor as he held out his hand to her. "Climb up, darling. I've been waiting for you."

Familiarity colored his voice as if he greeted an old friend. Nora knew she'd have remembered a dark-eyed hottie with curly hair and a wicked smile. Better yet, the bright green and yellow wagon he stood on was definitely memorable, especially with its fanciful drawings on the side and the two draft horses in the traces. Was she remembering part of a movie or a story Nana told her? That was it. Nana was part Romany Gypsy.

Still, it didn't make sense if she was in the story and the unknown man spoke English. Part of her wanted to take his hand and step up into the wagon to take off with him. At times, he looked into her eyes, not only as if he knew her, but also liked what he saw, which made his invitation tempting, very tempting.

The man dropped his hand. "Oh, I see you're still not ready, my Nora."

"How do you know my name?"

The man jumped down from the wagon, startling her, invading her space. His face filled her vision. She had to admire his strong jawline, and the crinkles around his eyes when he smiled caused her heart to beat faster. Her lips turned up naturally in response.

"Nora, Nora, how could you have forgotten me? I have loved you through several lifetimes and searched for you in each of mine. My life was desolate until I found you in a dream."

She was dreaming. That made sense.

"Nora, Nora."

Why did he keep repeating her name? He said her name as if he knew it well, without a blink or a hesitation, not like those fraternity guys trying to hit on her who could never quite remember her name, calling her everything from Nadine to Noreen. One even called her Norad, which she promptly informed him stood for North American Aerospace Defense Command. As she recalled, her would-be Romeo stumbled away, muttering, "bitch" loud enough for her to hear.

Men never worked too hard to romance her. Her purpose in attending college was to get an education, enabling her to obtain a decent job. A good portion of the girls who came to school felt the need to cut loose by skipping class, drinking too much, and having sex with guys they didn't know or couldn't remember. Often those same girls flunked out in less than two years. As a scholarship student, she needed to keep her grades up.

Why didn't she know his name?

His voice became higher, sounding more like a woman's, and he shook her shoulder vigorously. Why would he do that? Ogden would do that, but not this mysterious man.

"Nora, get up right now, or you're going to be late to your clinical."

Tonya's voice broke into her sleep-drugged thoughts. Her eyelids fluttered opened to the morning sunlight streaming around her curtain, indicating the time. "Oh, I overslept. Thank you, Tonya."

Her clean uniform hung on the hanger in front of her closet where she left it. The ironed smock and pants gave her a little reassurance that she'd make it on time. Some of the students showed up in wrinkled uniforms, and from standing too close to them, she suspected a few were unwashed, too. How could a person make it this far in the physician assistant program and still not take it seriously? Nora took it seriously. Of course, she did. She took everything too seriously, probably the curse of being the firstborn.

Tonya kept a running commentary as she dressed. "It's not like you to be late. I even heard your alarm go off, so I came into the room. You had a big, stupid grin on your face. Was it a good dream?"

Thinking back to the man in her dream, she'd probably call it perplexing as opposed to good. Yet, she was happy she'd remembered. Part of her recognized him and was glad to see him. "I guess you could call it a good dream."

"Ah ha." Tonya grinned and shook a finger at her. "I bet you weren't dreaming about Ogden then."

Grabbing a brush, she ran it through her short, dark hair. A shower would be better, but she'd given that up when she chose to continue to dream about the dark-eyed man instead of getting up on time. "How do you know I wasn't dreaming about Ogden?"

Snorting, her roommate shook her head. "Girl, now's not the time for it, but…"

Nora knew her outspoken roommate would say whatever was on her mind. Holding back wasn't her way. One of the things she enjoyed about the colorful friend. "Go on."

"All right, I will." Placing her long-fingered hands on her ample hips, she started, "We've been friends for almost four years, right?"

Nora nodded, thinking back to the day they ended up together. Her assigned roommate had reported her when she'd lighted a candle in recognition of the Goddess. It hadn't been the lighted candle, even though it was against the rules. Nope, her roommate had told her the Goddess statue creeped her out. Called her a Satanist then reported her for open flames. She should have reported Crystal for smoking in the bathroom, but she hadn't. Instead, in a panicked moment, she'd pictured her career and scholarship vanishing.

Luckily, she'd argued religious freedom and kept her scholarship but had had to move out of the dorm. Yeah, like, she'd had somewhere to go. Tonya, her anatomy lab partner, had asked why she'd missed class, and she'd explained the long story, not leaving anything out.

The usually jovial woman had grinned at the end of her story, instead of acting horrified as Nora had expected she would at the mention of the Goddess. "You and me, we belong together. My roommate found true love and is shacking up with her man. Could use help with the rent."

That had been that. Here they were, four years later. She knew good and well that Tonya would have her say. She earned the privilege by being the first, genuine friend Nora had had since Abby. "You know you saved me by inviting me to room with you."

"Don't you forget it. As your savior, I see how hard you work. Fun is not a part of your routine. Now, I know you are not a party-every-night girl, but you need to cut loose some time before you tie yourself to Ogden Thurston Graves The Third." Tonya pretended to shiver.

Sitting on her bed, Nora pulled on her socks and orthopedic white shoes. The shoes made her feel like a very unstylish sixty-year-old. "I know you don't like Ogden, but he's a brilliant resident. I am lucky to have him."

Tonya folded her arms. "Unlucky. The lucky-to-have-him nonsense sounds like something Ogden would say."

Actually, he did, but she'd never admit it to her roommate. "I need to hit the bathroom, then go." Suiting her actions to her words, she headed for the small bathroom they shared. One of Tonya's dates, after seeing the number of toiletries around the tub, had asked how many girls lived there.

Finished, she opened the bathroom door to find her friend waiting with a peanut butter sandwich. "Breakfast is the most important meal of the day."

Tonya had started out studying to be a nurse, but switched to nutritionist in her second year. Often, Nora benefitted from her concerns about proper diet. "Thanks."

Tonya followed her to the apartment building hallway to yell after her, "If Ogden is such a prize, why aren't those other nursing students all over him? Remember, a single doctor is still a premium commodity."

Jogging down the stairs, Nora tried to ignore the words. It was no secret that her friend didn't like Ogden. When he'd started coming around, she'd pretended he was helping her with her studies. It hadn't made sense that a busy resident would want to help a college student, but Tonya had marginally accepted her excuse. She'd still narrowed her eyes, muttering about Ogden being a poor excuse for a man.

The bus arrived, tabling her thoughts for a moment. Her bus pass was in the same hand as her sandwich. The bus driver gave her an annoyed look, but said nothing. She wouldn't be the first person to eat on the bus. At least she wouldn't leave her trash behind like the others. Spotting a pair of empty seats, she headed toward them, acknowledging a few of the other students on her way.

As she sank into the hard plastic seat, her shoulders relaxed. For the next twenty minutes, she could veg out and eat her sandwich. She turned her wrist to make sure the bus was on schedule, but her bare wrist mocked her attempt. Great, she'd forgotten her watch, which would make things infinitely more difficult. She used the second hand on her watch to count pulse rate. Dr. Benjamin pointed out that often you didn't have a blood pressure cuff nearby in an emergency. It paid to know how to take a pulse the old school way.

What else could she screw up this morning? Her breakfast disappeared in under two minutes with her rapid, angry bites taking out some of her aggravation on defenseless wheat bread. The sandwich left her thirsty and still hungry. No help for it. She should be grateful for what she had. That's how she felt about Ogden, even if other medical students or nurses weren't chasing him down. His prematurely balding head made him look older than his twenty-nine years, and she'd admit, he could be a bit stuffy talking about his Boston Brahman bloodline. Nora never said much about hers, not that he asked.

He'd told her once he decided on her because she showed the most intelligence among the students at the hospital. At the time, she'd thought that was high praise. It made her proud and happy. Later on, she'd realized he never said how pretty she was. Nope, not once. His interest was more in her genetics. He'd quizzed her on any pre-existing medical conditions and if any diseases ran in her family. For a brief moment, she wondered if he'd drop her if diabetes or, worse yet, dementia had shown up. On one level, she knew he would.

Still, he was a solid man, who was going places. A good person she could depend on. Although, sometimes, Ogden was the one who did all the depending, asking her to do things like pick up his dry cleaning, drop a snack by the hospital, or buy his mother a birthday present. At least it made her feel important. He did need her.

The familiar cityscape meant she was almost to the hospital. She glanced at the other bus riders, wondering what their lives were like. A few were students like her. Some were in whites, heading to the hospital, the same as her. Did any of the women expect a big romance in their lives? Some might. Maybe a few had one. Still, she didn't see that for herself, not after what had happened in high school.

She bit her bottom lip, trying to block the memory the best she could. Not remembering helped her to cope. Unlike her little sister, Leah, she'd chosen not to be secretive about her faith. If people could wear crosses and printed shirts proclaiming them hipsters for Christ, she was unsure why she couldn't wear a simple pentacle. She had for a short while, until she started to hear the rumors that she and her friends had kinky witchy sex.

Her fists closed, causing her nails to bite into her palms. Scenes from that horrific night flashed into her mind. The football players, her friend Abby screaming, the boys holding her down, mocking her with their boozy slurs as they penetrated her. The incident, as she preferred to call it, was all a horrible nightmare she worked to forget. She blamed herself. Maybe if she hadn't felt she'd had something to prove, she and Abby wouldn't have suffered the unjust consequences.

The day after Abby flipped out and refused to communicate with anyone, Nora drove to the clinic alone. Abby's father freaked when he heard the names of the players that she recognized. Said they were the offspring of the local movers and shakers and ordinary people had no defense against them. Nora decided to say nothing as she drove to the clinic for pregnancy and STD testing. Luckily, the tests came back negative. The helpful nurse had lectured her on the dangers of STDs, and how even though a person could have an STD, you didn't always contract it. She'd warned against making the mistake about thinking the person was clean. Nora doubted those football players were clean by a long shot.

Ironically, the incident—as horrible as it had been—had made her consider nursing as a career choice. When she'd needed help, that one nurse had given her practical advice without judging her. She wanted to help other people when they needed help.

Technically, she both knew she should have reported the attack. Unfortunately, since the kinky witchy sex rumors had existed before the incident, she'd doubted anyone would have believed her. The attack had been premeditated, which made it somehow worse.

She'd never told anyone as she waited for some online tell-all, but it never came. Unable to stop them from ravishing her body, she'd cursed them, long and lavishly, using everything she'd ever read in spell books, threatening them if they ever breathed a word. She also knew she wasn't supposed to wish ill on people or it would come back on her threefold.

The depraved, sadistic males who'd jumped her and Abby were human garbage with fancy haircuts and expensive clothes. She could accept that, but still couldn't figure out why they'd picked her and Abby. It wasn't exactly like they were the school skanks. It could have been a crime of opportunity, except the rumors about the witchy sex started before the attack occurred.

Her family had moved shortly after the incident. She was sure no one knew, but the timing of the move was suspicious. She never found out if anything bad had happened to the boys. They did lose every football game for the rest of the season, but she doubted that had been from a curse.

Worse, though, Abby had gone to a home for the mentally ill after having a breakdown. Nora was able to see her, but all her friend did was look off into the distance, retreating so far into herself, she shut out the world around her.

Nora's way of dealing was to give up on the idea of romance. Maybe the idea of love worked out for some people, such as her mother, but not for her. Those handsome, cocky males just wanted to do vicious, cruel acts to her body. The passionate romance scenes with the couple carried away with each other were not for her. In fact, she avoided those movies.

Ogden wasn't the type to inspire grand passion, and she preferred that. Not like her dream stranger, who made her heart beat fast and her hands sweat. Not a good sign, but luckily he didn't exist.

"I'm hurt, my darling, that you would malign me so by saying I don't exist."

She cut her eyes to the empty seat beside her and the window next to her. There were no other places the voice could have come from, but her mind. Must be the sleeping pill she took last night. Perhaps she fell asleep on the way to the hospital. That was it.

The bus stopped. Students and a nurse stood to disembark. Nora joined them, anxious to get the day started and her mind off the past and the sexy male voice whispering inside her skull. According to her psychology classes, her personality could have fractured due to the incident. Such a coping mechanism would allow different aspects to take charge to protect her from future harm. There were a few flaws with the theory.

The elderly security guard called out a cheery hello.

"Morning, Herman," she responded.

The fact the hospital had guards at every door had surprised her at first, until she learned that the inner-city hospital was a favorite haunt for homeless folks or those sleeping off a drunk on the long vinyl couches in the lobby. Some less attentive, or perhaps more compassionate, guards allowed a few homeless in to pass the night, especially during the winter.

People crowded around the elevator. Nora headed for the stairs. The exercise would be good and would allow her time to think about the voice.

It couldn't be a coping mechanism. If so, why wait five years to show up? By this time, she was over it. The voice didn't represent some part of her or speak for her. No, it addressed her. Her workload, coupled with her schooling, could be the root. Tonya planting ideas in her head as to why Ogden wasn't right for her didn't help. No wonder this sexy stranger populated her dreams and thoughts. He was the exact opposite of Ogden.

By the third floor, she was rethinking her plan to climb to the fifth floor. No use, she needed to get to class on time. Her mind put up the image of Ogden next to her dream man, almost as if she were examining a textbook. The mystery man exuded charm and a lilting Irish accent, while Ogden held no claim to any type of charm, but did have a haughty way of pronouncing certain words. He often informed her he was saying the words the correct way, implying everyone else wasn't. When the mystery man jumped down to stand beside her, she saw he was a couple of inches taller than her five-foot-seven, and his wide shoulders tapered down to a narrow waist and a flat stomach. Her only regret was she hadn't notice more in her dream. Ogden loomed over her at six-foot-one. Despite his height, he lacked the muscle tone a person might expect from a tall man. He was already developing a potbelly, as well, not that she'd ever mention it aloud.

The fifth-floor door finally appeared. Nora pushed it open with a grateful gasp. A chattering group of students exited the elevator at the same time she entered the hallway. Some were juggling coffee and a doughnut. Envy jabbed her at their casual attitude and capricious spending. She knew good and well that coffee and a doughnut at the hospital would run almost five dollars. No telling how many peanut butter sandwiches she could eat compared to that empty calorie snack. Still, she sighed a little. It would have been nice not to count every penny. Soon, she'd be making money and could buy doughnuts if she wished, not that Tonya would approve if they were still roommates.

Rushing to catch up with the others, she almost ran into Ogden. Her almost-boyfriend glared down at her.

"There you are, Nora. I've waited"—he checked his watch—"almost eight minutes for you to show. I made a special trip to this floor to say hello. I am a busy man."

"Sorry." The apology popped out of her mouth before she even thought about it. What did she have to be sorry about? She'd spent the last thirty minutes of her life to get here. Her welcome was a morning scolding she could do without. "Hello. Now you can go back to your important stuff."

Ogden threw her a bewildered look before he walked away without comment.

In another man, his behavior might be insulting. Unfortunately, this was his normal behavior. A smirk crossed her face. He hadn't even recognized her sarcasm. Yep, his "important stuff" included telling the other residents why they were wrong in their diagnoses. Often, he acted as if he were the teaching doctor.

Another female student caught up with her as she walked to the briefing room. The redheaded woman grimaced before commenting, "Did God tell you that you weren't wearing your uniform right?"

Nora automatically gave the woman a slight smile while she mentally took inventory of the woman's uniform. Clean, ironed, a little tight. Still, that wasn't a big deal. Weight tended to fluctuate in college. It certainly didn't merit buying a new uniform, especially on a student's budget. "Yours looks fine. He told me I was late."

Her companion rolled her eyes. "What is he, your father or husband? I'm unsure why the man has such an inflated opinion of himself. Word is he's annoyed most of the female students with unwanted comments."

Nora's eyebrows shot up. She'd never heard anything about this before. "Um, I didn't catch your name. Mine's Nora Carpenter."

"Katie Marshall." The woman nodded at a handsome intern who returned her interest. "He's a cutie, but I heard he has a nurse on the third floor. You'd think as students that we get first chance at the doctors, but no. Even that officious boar you were talking to has a woman. Imagine that."

"Oh, really." Nora pretended some mild interest. "Didn't you just tell me he was flirting with all the female students?"

Tinkling laughter filled the air as Katie's face contorted in mirth. She stopped a moment for a breath, before answering. "I didn't say flirting. He feels free to make comments to all the females, from their uniforms or hair not being right to criticizing their chart notes. He's a chauvinist. Never says a word to the male students. He's probably afraid one of them would punch him out for his *help*."

The fact he never criticized the men said a great deal. Ogden must feel some natural superiority over all women. That didn't bode well for their future life together.

She entered the classroom and edged her way to the front to hear better and have a good view of the whiteboard, where Dr. Benjamin stood with a marker in her hand. Nora grabbed a front-row seat.

The female doctor spoke fast and did not tolerate slowpokes or whiners, a woman Nora could understand. The doctor began going over the various signs of diabetes before everyone had sat down. A pointed look landed on the students still consuming their doughnuts.

Nora took rapid notes in her notebook. Most of the information she already knew, but she still took notes. It wouldn't hurt to refresh her knowledge. Besides, Dr. Benjamin might mention something new.

One part of her mind dwelled on what Katie had said. The woman certainly was outspoken, but it didn't mean she'd lied. It gave her something to consider. Life with Ogden became less and less desirable with each day and each ridiculous demand and pouting behavior when she refused to do his piddly errands. Didn't he care that her life was busy? She didn't even have a car. How was she supposed to run all over town for him? Why was she dating him, anyhow?

"Ms. Carpenter, would you suspect diabetes in a patient losing weight rapidly?"

The doctor's voice jolted her out of her contemplation. "I would, but I would ask about other symptoms, including feeling thirst, bruising easily, and a continual sense of fatigue."

"Very good." The doctor gave her an approving look before moving on to another likely target.

Nora doubted she would be so approving if the woman knew she was analyzing her love life. "Love life" was certainly the wrong term. She doubted if there was any love between the two of them. They used each other for different purposes.

Ironically, Ogden probably thought she enjoyed the prestige of being his girlfriend. There was no honor connected with it. Embarrassment would better sum up her feelings. She hadn't mentioned to Katie that she was disparaging her man. Instead, she was curious to see what others thought, which was pretty much as she'd suspected. Still, it hit her in the face like a splash of cold water on a winter day. If she were honest with herself, she'd admit Ogden was her wall. He served as a barrier against other men's flirtatious banter. When she'd first started school, she'd frozen out the potential Romeos with her aloof manner. The tactic earned her the label of Ice Queen and made a few work that much harder, usually after they had three or four beers in them. A boyfriend was Tonya's solution, but her roommate never suspected she'd pick a pretentious bore.

Ogden wasn't as much of a deterrent as she thought he'd be. Since he wasn't on campus, men tended to believe he was mythical or of no importance. Nor, despite his size, did the man intimidate. He also did not show any type of possessiveness toward her, unless it was when he wanted his errands run first.

By the end of the lecture, Nora decided that a future with Ogden might not be in her best interest. For now, she'd let things drift. It was easier that way.

Chapter Two

Nora slid into the staff lounge to grab a break. The day had gone faster than she'd expected while she'd taught a mother and her recently diagnosed daughter how to check the child's blood sugar. Children shouldn't get diseases. It almost made her tear up watching the eight-year-old bite her lip as she bravely pricked her finger. The doctor would monitor the child's progress before recommending an insulin pump.

Nora's mind galloped ahead, imagining the young girl trying to eat a balanced diet while her friends gobbled fast food and sugary treats. It would be hard to resist. They had plenty of adults on the diabetic floor who couldn't resist overindulging in treats that could kill them, or at least put them in the hospital.

Discipline is what it took. She'd tried to explain this to the over-emotional mother that it would help if the mother cleaned up the entire family's diet, eliminating foods that might cause her daughter to secretly binge. Mom might do it for a few weeks, or maybe not at all, declaring that it wouldn't be fair to the rest of the family. People say they want to help a loved one, but seldom are willing to deprive themselves of a likable activity.

It frustrated her to see families reeking of smoke gathered around a lung-cancer patient. Alcoholics suffering from cancer of the liver rarely had to buy liquor, since it often was already in the house or friends delivered it.

Her hands fisted. She could not make family members realize they played a significant part in their loved one's ability to heal. Her own family helped her to heal in their own way. Of course, they didn't ask her about her lack of dates. Her father believed academics came first and approved. Her mother made a few hints about boys her age at various gatherings they attended, but never pushed her. Nana never said anything, but gave her the eye as if she knew. Her family believed Nana had *the sight,* which would explain her amulet.

Her hand went up to grasp the necklace she always wore. The amulet consisted of agate, galena, tiger-eye, chiastolite, and malachite. Each protection stone swung from a circle, which represented feminine power. She never took it off despite one of her clinical supervisors implying it was germ-ridden and inappropriate. Instead, she wore it tucked under her clothing. No worries about her wearing anything low-cut enough to expose the necklace or her cleavage.

If that wasn't enough, Nana also had given her an anklet composed of healing stones to wear. The delicate chain connected citrine, crystal, and ametrine. Crystal was a magnifier, while the other two were for depression. Often, when she'd returned from school those first weeks after the incident, the scent of sage lingered in her room. No doubt, her grandmother and mother were smudging her room, clearing it of negativity. The more she thought about it, the more she believed she hadn't conquered her fear and depression on her own.

Maybe Abby wouldn't have been in the mental health center if her family knew how to help her. It puzzled her, though, if Nana knew and hadn't insisted on calling the police and reporting the boys. Then again, Nana's ability probably allowed her to see nothing would happen to the popular boys, while Nora would suffer humiliation and harassment. Even if evidence stared the police in the face, they'd still doubt.

Sometimes, Nora wondered if there was an instinctive response for men to believe men and distrust women. Hard to say, but she did know she had a tendency to distrust men. Often, she questioned the simplest actions by males, trying to decide if they meant her harm. Sure, there were decent men in her life, including her father, little brother, and a few of her instructors. The fact that she'd developed friendships with Brian and Damien, fellow students, was a plus, though them being gay may have been a factor.

What if her life were more normal?

Maybe it was. According to statistics presented in trauma medicine class, one out of four women suffered a sexual assault at the hands of someone they knew. Out of these assaults, only three percent ever resulted in jail time. The number of rapes rose with the use of rape drugs and inferences that the woman wanted it. How did the other women get past it? Did they have one true love who demonstrated how a relationship should be? No doubt, many men would break up with the woman unsure how to deal with the situation.

The door opened, admitting a few residents. Nora looked at the two young men who'd entered. Neither was Ogden, solidifying her decision to leave. Caution warned her not to allow herself to be alone with multiple men.

One of the men glanced at her and smiled. His nameplate read T. Mangano. His curly hair reminded her of her mystery man.

"Don't leave on our account," Mangano said. He held out his hand. "My name is Terrence."

Nora gingerly took his hand, not wanting to touch him, and gave it a single firm pump, meeting social protocol. "No problem. My break is over anyhow."

Nora pulled the door shut behind her, but not before she heard the other man chide his friend. "Real smooth, Terrence, chased her off before you even got her name."

No reason to linger to hear his response, but part of her wanted to. Call it feminine curiosity. She thought she'd detected an actual desire to meet her. Tonya often reminded her that her aloofness pulled in men more than any outright flirting. What a shame, Tonya concluded, when she didn't want to attract them. No one could accuse her of being friendly to the residents. She treaded a thin line, between civility and abruptness.

Wasn't it enough she'd cut her hair, making it into a dark cap? After the incident, she'd used a pair of scissors to shear off the locks that had provided a handhold for the football players. Her mother had cleaned up the ravaged hair and oddly never asked why Nora had done it, only sighed a little at the loss of her long hair.

Close to the end of her day, she glanced at the wall clock. A group of students headed toward the elevators. She'd joined them when she saw Ogden making his way down the hall. Without any conscious thought, she worked her way through the group to be the first to board the elevator. As the doors closed, she breathed a sigh of relief, thinking she'd avoided another errand. A smitten man would have raced down the stairs to meet the elevator, as a fellow student's beau did once. Ogden would not rush down the stairs to greet her. Good, because he'd meet her with a pout instead of a smile.

On the bus, she watched the familiar scenery flash by. Even though her eyes threatened to close, she had to stay alert or she'd miss her work stop. Her short-order-cook position allowed her both lunch and dinner, which was a measure in savings. As a cook, she didn't have to flirt with all the men who thought they were handsome or witty. Nora heard the servers' complaints about too-friendly patrons and blessed her skill to cook several meals at once.

After carrying her backpack into the restaurant, she changed into her cook whites. It seemed ridiculous to change from white clothes to white clothes, but she needed to keep her hospital clothes spotless. Once she became associated with a hospital or doctor's office, she'd have more variety in what she could wear. Until then, it was all whites, so the students were easy to pick out. Of course, the patients couldn't differentiate between actual staff and students and often asked her for assistance.

Dressed in her cook clothes, she was welcomed by the scent of frying onions and the first shift cook's enthusiastic greeting as she pushed open the swinging door.

"Thank God, you're here." Ernie motioned to her with a spatula. "Get your apron on."

Nora stopped to clock in at the time clock. She was ten minutes early for her shift. She perched the silly envelope hat on her head and wrapped the oversized apron around her slender body. "What's up?"

Ernie flipped a series of burgers before answering. "Legionnaires convention."

Nora reached for a long-handled spatula and started pushing the onions around. "Why didn't they head over to that girlie place with the wide-screen television?"

Ernie gave her an unreadable look before answering. "Their food is horrible, while Order Up is best known for quality."

Odd, that's not what she'd heard about the small restaurant. Its popularity stemmed from being open all night and being right next to a huge hotel. Eventually, the guests tired of paying twelve dollars for a burger and made the short trip. She didn't correct the man, especially if he took pride in his work.

Ernie grinned at her. "I was joking. I doubt their hearts could take the other place since their average age is eighty."

"Oh." Nora stored the information. Too much stimulation could kill an elderly man. Then again, Ernie could be messing with her. It wouldn't be the first time. He insisted one of their regulars had a crush on her. The middle-aged man he'd referred to had cold, light blue eyes and always wanted to talk to the chef about his meal.

The first couple of times she'd talked to him, there had been nothing wrong with her cooking, and she'd known it. The man's complaints had put her on the defensive, causing her to barrel through the swinging doors, much to his delight. One time he'd complimented the food while his eyes roamed over her body, making her cook whites feel filthy by the interaction. Why couldn't he have been satisfied with Bonnie, the waitress, who always wore her smock unzipped to the point of being R-rated? Evil had rolled off the man. She'd looked at the other people in the restaurant. None of them had seen him for what he was, only her. He'd known it, too, which was probably why he'd complained, knowing she could do nothing. It had made her feel helpless—not a feeling she liked.

Sometimes, the servers ran interference for her, saying she was too busy or could make him another meal if it wasn't to his liking. He never accepted a new meal. A pattern began to develop. He showed up only on the days she worked. How he knew, when she worked perplexed her, since her off days changed. It made her wonder if he watched her or waited somewhere close by for her to show up for work before entering the diner. The good news was he didn't show up every day, and he didn't always complain when he did.

Ernie knew the man made her uncomfortable. There was nothing she could do about it since he was a regular customer. He never raised his voice or used threatening language. Occasionally, he'd say something bizarre along with his usual complaints. Once he offered to bring in a sample of sauerkraut that he'd made. Her creepy feeling appeared to be just hers. The manager, Barb, had laughed at her fears and told her she was a pretty girl who could cook, which was what all men wanted.

Linda, an older waitress, stuck her head in the kitchen window. "Ernie, getting any closer on those burger plates?"

Nora arranged the bun and fixings on the plates as Ernie argued with Linda good-naturedly. A ding of the deep fryer sent her to the fries table as Ernie slid the burgers onto the plate.

Linda called her name, causing to Nora to peer over her shoulder. "Hey, Nora, you are here. Well, I'll be. He was right,"

"Right about what?" She tore open another bag of fries and poured them into the fryer basket. Her hand lingered on the basket for a second as she debated about starting them.

"Your fan told me you were here, back in the kitchen. I told him your shift hadn't started yet. Goes to show how much attention I was paying when a customer knows more of what is going on than I do."

Linda's words caused the basket to slip out of her hand into the hot oil with a loud sputtering fall. Her body jerked back in reflex to avoid the heated oil. Great, not what she wanted to hear. Today appeared to be populated with troublesome males, from her dream man, Ogden's moodiness and demands, overfriendly interns, and her resident stalker. Maybe she was just paranoid. The man probably lived alone and thought of the people at the diner as his family. If so, she didn't want to know what family member she played.

The back door opened, catching her attention as the milk deliveryman backed into the area with his milk crates-laden hand truck. She abandoned her place at the fryer to hold the door open. The graying hair peeking out from the cap identified Otis.

Her first thought on meeting Otis two years ago had been that at his age he shouldn't be delivering milk. He had to be older than her grandparents were. The sweet-natured man had told her he was grateful someone would give an old man a job. Still, she felt obligated to help as much as she could to give the man a break. Originally, it was a battle. Otis was very old school and didn't believe females should lift heavy milk crates. Luckily, she'd managed to get him to change his mind. She waved goodbye, and before she returned to her work at the prep counter, Ernie made an up and down wave motion with his hand, and then held up four fingers.

Nora laughed before reaching into the freezer for fish fillets. Ernie had made up his own system for relaying information when he thought the kitchen might be too loud. His system relied on someone looking at him first to be effective. Nora never pointed out the flaw. Most of the time, the cooks worked alone, unless it was busy like today. She dropped the fish, jiggled the fries, and then began to put out a series of plates.

She glanced back to the exterior door. "Ernie, do they always keep the back door unlocked for deliveries?"

The man's eyebrows lowered. "How long you worked here?"

Nora had landed the job when she was sophomore. "About three years."

Ernie nodded in agreement. "You asking me something you already know." He rolled his eyes and snorted a little in disgust. "Cheese, four."

Nora placed the cheese slices on the burgers, wishing she hadn't mentioned the door, but lately it worried her. Ernie was right that the door had been unlocked for as long as she'd worked there. "I know, but it doesn't seem safe. What about late at night?"

The smell of hamburgers made her stomach growl. She'd be able to sneak a burger once they slowed down. It was amazing she hadn't gained weight at this job. Tonya joked that she'd have to slow down for weight to catch up to her.

Ernie slid the cheeseburgers on the buns and nodded in the direction of the fries at the same time the buzzer went off. Carrying the plates to the fries area, she mounded shoestring potatoes on the plates. Generous servings kept the customers coming back. Tonya referred to it as maximizing heart attack risk.

As if remembering her question, Ernie replied, "I think they lock the door around ten, because no deliveries will come later than that."

It made sense. She'd worked the third shift only a few times, and she couldn't remember locking the door. That meant she'd worked with the unlocked door all night. Anyone could have come in and easily pulled her out of the building or into the walk-in freezer where her screams wouldn't be heard. A shiver vibrated through her, causing her hands to grasp the counter for support.

"Hey, are you worried about someone stealing our bacon?" Ernie laughed at his comment. "Heard about two guys taking a forklift and stealing six hundred pounds of bacon. They must have really liked bacon, right?"

"Right." She held her hands out. They appeared steady, which made it safe to carry the plates to the pass-through window. "Linda, four cheeseburger plates," she called out.

After setting the plates down, Nora pulled off Linda's order paper and placed it on the spike. Order Up held to old-school ways because they were cheap. Oddly, they seemed effective, too. No one stopped working if the computer went down. She scanned the room to see if Linda had heard her and caught him looking at her.

Their eyes met, and he smiled a genuine glad-to-see-you smile.

Nora spun away, refusing to acknowledge him. He'd told her once his name was Neal. Did she expect him to call him by his name as if they were friends? Her nametag identified her. She hoped Linda would make it to the window in a timely fashion to pick up her order. No way would she stand there calling her name while Neal tried to make friendly.

The rest of the shift was uneventful. Ernie stayed an extra hour and a half, which allowed Nora time to stand in the kitchen to wolf down a cheeseburger. The servers received one meal with their shift, while cooks received two. Ernie said it was because they didn't get tips. It was probably more based on not being able to monitor what a cook ate, so you might as well give them two meals. The only problem was Board of Health restrictions against eating in the kitchen. Cooks across the country managed to skirt this by not eating while health inspectors were there.

Brandon, the night cook, came in around seven to hang out and eat before his shift. The bald-headed cook was a former Marine, sporting several patriotic tattoos. Nora imagined if someone made the mistake of sneaking in the back door when Brandon was working, he'd leave quickly once he saw the muscle-bound man.

Business had slowed enough that after she fixed him food, she left the kitchen to talk to him. Oddly, she felt at ease with the intimidating man. There was no aura of evil around him.

"Thanks for the omelet." Brandon delivered the praise after his first bite. "You have a nice light hand with the eggs. Know when to fold before it browns too much."

Her face flushed a little. People didn't normally compliment her cooking. They only griped when they thought it wasn't fast enough. "Thanks. It's just eggs, ya know."

He shoveled in another mouthful, chewed then swallowed before speaking. "Yeah, but you'd be surprised how the average person can't make a decent egg. Either they break the yolk or end up burning it."

Nora found herself smiling at his simple praise. In another man, she might have thought he was flirting with her, but this was Brandon. She felt she'd known him forever, as opposed to just the last three years. "I think you're just saying it to make me feel good."

He grinned. The simple gesture made him look younger. How old was he? Maybe in his thirties, hard to know with his shaved head.

He's not for you.

Blinking, Nora looked around to see if anyone else had entered the diner. Nope, it was still just her, Brandon, and Bonnie. That meant the voice had been in her head.

"Did I make you feel good?" Brandon asked with a wink. "If so, great, but the eggs really are good. What do you want me to make you for your meal?"

She started to ask for a BLT. Should she be wasting time eating when she was hearing voices in her head? "I'm real beat. I think I will go straight home and sleep."

"Tell you what," Brandon said, glancing in Bonnie's direction, "go make yourself a grilled cheese, write up a ticket, and take it home with you."

The restaurant had a cardinal rule about no food going home with employees. It had seemed ridiculous at first, when the workers already got a free meal, but one meal could easily morph into four.

"Okay," she mouthed, returning to the kitchen to make herself the sandwich she'd been thinking about earlier. It would be a secret just between her and Brandon. Before she went to sleep tonight, she'd eat it while she covered the chapter on infectious diseases. Hard to believe people still die from the flu. She tucked the sandwich in her backpack.

Brandon came into the kitchen while she was tidying up. "Nora, stop cleaning. There will be nothing for me to do in the wee hours of the night."

She put the rag she'd used to wipe down the counter into the dishwasher tray for sterilization. "Okay. Are you good, then? I'll head out."

Brandon placed his arms behind him on the counter, causing his biceps to bunch up. The man definitely had muscles, probably lifted in his spare time. "I'm good."

She turned away, thinking for the briefest second that the words were a double entendre. It almost felt like something had changed between the two of them. That couldn't be. She grabbed her bag and headed for the bus stop.

Brandon followed behind her. "I don't like you waiting for the bus in the dark."

Gesturing to the streetlight and the bench outside the diner window, she said, "You can see me from in here."

He crossed his arms. "That's what I intend to do, then."

Nora waved at Bonnie sitting at the counter counting her tips. Instead of waving back, the woman shot her a peculiar look. Had she entered an alternate universe where no one seemed to act normal?

Shouldering her bag, she walked to the stop. The headlights of the bus announced its arrival, along with a belch of diesel smoke and a mechanical grumble of gears. Turning slightly before she got on the bus, she noticed Brandon watching with his arms folded. He put one hand up when he saw her glance back. She waved in return.

Stepping on the bus, she ran her pass through before collapsing onto the nearest seat. Inside the diner, she could see Bonnie talking to Brandon. His eyes were on the bus and not on the server who often beefed up her tips with her flirtatious manner and revealing cleavage.

What part of "not for you" did you not understand?

The voice again.

Please, she couldn't break down so close to graduation. She'd get home, get some sleep, maybe, review the chapter in the morning. Yes, that's what she'd do, and everything would be better in the morning.

CHAPTER THREE

Tonya called out a greeting from the kitchen as Nora staggered into the apartment. Exhausted, Nora simply said, "I'm beat. Going to bed."

The smell of cinnamon and cayenne pepper lingered in the hallway. A curious combination. Normally, she'd investigate what new concoction her roommate had in development. Tonya's passion consisted of putting together nutritional and yummy foods to tempt the palate. This time it wasn't enough to keep Nora from bed.

A quick shower would strip most of the grease from her body and remove the smell of onions.

Later, in bed with her eyes closed, the image of the curly-haired charmer returned. Maybe she'd dream of him. It certainly would be better than her creepy diner fan. Her entire body stiffened at the unwelcome thought.

Dear sweet Goddess, do not let me dream of Mr. Icky.

Comforted by the short prayer, her body relaxed as she drifted into slumber.

Trees surrounded her, and the smell of campfire smoke drifted toward her. Nora gazed at the surrounding trees and the late afternoon sun. Evening approached, and she was wandering in unfamiliar woods? Why had she come? Couldn't exactly call her a nature girl and she avoided going places where she'd be alone and at risk. Walking through a forest alone at almost dark was foolhardy, serving as the beginning to several horror movies. It was right up there with the ones featuring the too-stupid-to-live females who investigated a noise they heard in the basement after the power went out and armed with nothing more than a flashlight, despite knowing a serial killer was on the loose in the area.

She always considered herself a cautious female, especially after the incident. What was she doing in the woods?

The nearby crack of a branch snapping sent her heart into her throat. The self-defense classes came to mind. A pat to her side revealed no purse to swing like a battle mace or keys to scour her attacker's face, which left her with nothing in the way of defensive tools.

A branch about as long as her arm lay near her feet. Picking it up, she gave it a few experimental swings. It would do since she didn't see anything else. Another twig snap and the rustle of dry leaves had her crouching into a defensive pose to minimize her height and widening her stance for good balance. Her fingers wrapped around the stick as she waited. More rustling, and then the culprit casually strolled into view… with her child. A delicate doe with a fawn stepped through the trees, checking every green plant for edibility. The acceptable ones merited a nibble, while a few others didn't. The fawn followed close to its mother's side. A glance in Nora's direction caused it to crowd up against its mother. She'd frightened it. The doe and fawn were so beautiful.

"Not as beautiful as you, my love," a voice whispered into her ear.

She whirled, slashing with her impromptu wooden weapon. The stick snapped against the man's shoulder, not even causing him to stagger.

The man from her previous dream grinned at her as he brushed off the wooden bits sticking to his embroidered vest. "Now, my sweet Nora, is that any way to greet your beloved?"

"You are not my beloved," she said, stomping her foot a little. Why did this man insist on flirting with her? She didn't flirt. Her eyes flickered down to her broken stick. "Why didn't my stick hurt you?"

The man pressed a hand to his heart and stumbled back a few steps. "It's hurting you're after, is it? We have yet to exchange any cross words." He squatted and picked up a piece of broken branch to examine.

Nora observed the man, but more important, she cataloged her reactions. The fear, which caused her to break out in a cold sweat and shift into a fight-or-flight mode, vanished. Her heart slowed down, but it was still beating a little fast. Certainty that she had nothing to fear from him filled her, odd in itself since she'd been on guard against every unknown man for the last four years. It had taken her four months before she'd relaxed her guard around Brandon, who seemed to be truly a decent person.

The man rose to his feet, brandishing the small portion of the stick. "Your stick was more hollow than wood. Termites worked it good." He handed it to her.

In the fading light, Nora could see tiny holes riddled the branch. The thought of termites made her drop the branch quickly. The man laughed a low, pleasant laugh that somehow managed to warm her insides. Curious, it was hard to explain the sensation she'd never felt before. Maybe she had but had forgotten.

"Never fear the termites, Nora. They are the forest's gardener, helping things to grow. I am just getting ready to eat my supper and would be pleased to have you join me." He gestured to the drifting smoke.

An appetizing scent overrode the smoke aroma. Her stomach growled, embarrassing her and making her aware that she'd never eaten the sandwich in her backpack. "All right. You walk. I'll follow."

Maybe the man made her feel safe, but she hadn't lost all her sense. Better to have him in front of her. She watched as he gracefully slipped through the trees. No wonder she hadn't heard him sneak up on her. A part of her she'd suspected was dead, or at least dormant, appreciated the width of his shoulders, the straight back, and the very fine buttocks filling out his trousers. Interesting that she'd noticed. Even more, she could feel her body reacting.

Her fingers drifted to her neck to calculate her pulse. It kicked up some, not out of fear, though.

The man looked over his shoulder, and their eyes caught. Her fingers still on her throat caught the jump in her heartbeat.

"Are you coming, darling?" His voice, warm with promise, carried a hint of laughter.

Nora found herself smiling. How strange. She almost never smiled at men, because it could be considered an invitation. Odd that she'd ended up in a relationship with Ogden. Then again, "relationship" might be a misleading term. She ran errands for him while using their association as a shield to keep other men away. Their physical relationship was almost non-existent. Ogden was not a hand-holder or casual kisser. He never pushed her for sex, which made him the ideal pretend boyfriend. The peculiar affiliation kept her safe from the wild emotional swings other women experienced when involved with men. She also believed it erected a barrier around her that other men dared not try to pass. Her interaction with various men had proved that wasn't always the case.

The man regarded her with patient and amused eyes. "Are you holding your head on? Was it about to tumble off your swan-like neck?"

He thought he was a funny one. "I was taking my pulse. It's when you—"

"I know what taking a pulse is. That's one of the reasons I need you here—to help with the sickness." He held her arm and helped her over a fallen log.

Illness she understood. "How can I help?" She considered his hand on her elbow. She had never been one to take assistance, even as a child. As the oldest, she felt the need to do everything on her own. She was a trailblazer of sorts. No one told her she had to, unless you counted her inner voice. No reason she couldn't have scampered across the log on her own, but she appreciated the gesture.

"What's your name? You keep calling me by my mine, but never mentioned yours."

"My sainted grandmother would have my head if she saw my poor manners." Holding on to her hand, he led her to two fallen logs bordering the fire. "Your chaise, my lady."

He sat on the other log and used a long-handled spoon to stir the pot suspended over the fire. "I am Clayton McFane. I supposed I expected you to recognize me since we have loved each other for several lifetimes. The first few were a little rocky, but once we got the sense of one another as soul mates, we came together quite well." A grin brightened his face as his eyes flickered up, demonstrating he was recalling times gone by.

Make that, times he thought had gone by. Nora wasn't all that sure she believed they'd known each other for lifetimes. Still, she'd witnessed both her sister and grandfather transported through time, as easily as if only going to the next city for shopping.

Her nana swore she and Grandpa Buell were soul mates. There was also something reassuring about Clayton.

Placing her hands on the log, she leaned back and stretched her legs toward the fire. Her cartoon pajama pants looked wildly out of place in the woodland setting. You'd think she would have picked out something more appropriate to wear in her dream.

Clayton ladled the fragrant stew into a bowl.

"Clayton," she started, earning a smile for using his name. "How come you know me and where I was?"

"Oh, that." He straightened and walked toward her, carrying the bowl. "Granny McFane claims I have a touch of the fey about me. That's why I often know things that are going to happen." He presented the bowl to her, along with a spoon. "Eat."

Nora dug into the stew thick with potatoes, chunks of meat, and gravy. The taste resonated on her tongue with the right blend of spices. Tonya would have appreciated the dish. She closed her eyes and savored the flavor before swallowing.

"I'd count myself a happy man if I put that expression on your face instead of my rabbit stew," Clayton murmured the words close by, causing her eyelids to pop open.

Nora didn't know what to say to what was clearly flirtatious remark. Instead, she ate more stew, even though the thought of rabbit made it harder to choke down the meat.

Clayton intertwined his fingers and gazed down at them as he spoke. "I've been warned that a person doesn't force fate's hand. I'd be agreeing with that, except, if fate didn't want you to be here, you wouldn't be."

His bit of cracked reasoning had her almost choking on a potato. A hearty back slap sent the errant vegetable airborne. Blinking, she looked into Clayton's concerned face. The firelight did nothing to negate the strong lines of his face or the lively blue eyes. Handsome he might be, but there was also sincerity, a sense of compassion that she often found lacking in twenty-first-century males. "How did you find me?"

His hand stroked his chin. "Well, I tell ya, it was no simple matter. I am growing older every day. I am nigh on to thirty-three."

Nora pretended to be horrified. "That old?"

Taking her pretense for real, he nodded his head gravely. "Yes, that old, and there'd been no sign of my soul mate, despite my looking. I dreamt you were in America, but unfortunately the time I was unclear on. I left Ireland in search of you."

Nora stirred her delicious stew, debating if she could eat any more of it knowing it was composed of creatures she was more used to seeing singing and dancing in children's movies. "That doesn't answer my question of how you find me."

He lifted his eyebrows. "I see you haven't changed much. Still demanding answers. I did some divination magick. Much to my horror, I found we were in two different centuries, both alone. This I found hard to accept. At night when my loneliness was at its peak, I searched for you across time, calling your name. Did you ever have a sense of me?"

"Well, at first I would say no, but lately yes. Your voice is in my head, making me wonder if I am losing my mind. I noticed it because it sounds like you and not my own internal musings. Why is that?"

Nora placed the forgotten bowl on the log. Clayton picked it up and stirred the stew before taking a bite that he obviously relished before finishing the rest in four rapid bites. He went back to the pot to dip up more food.

Noticing her attention on the bowl, he explained, "I have only one bowl. I know I should have bartered for another, but I wasn't too sure if I could bring you across. Even now you are here only on the strength of my will and need." He dug his spoon back into his bowl.

The idea that he could just snatch her out of time should have frightened her. Instead, it mesmerized her with possibilities. "Could I just pull Napoleon or Ben Franklin out of time if I chose?"

Clayton looked reflective as he chewed. "I'm no expert on these matters. I believe there needs to be a connection or a bond between two individuals to draw them to one another. We've had lifetimes to build the connections. You are the first person I ever brought through time. Unfortunately, you stayed only briefly before." He placed his bowl on the ground as he leaned slightly toward her, placing both hands on his knees.

"You brought me over before?" The memory of him jumping down from the wagon came to mind.

"I have. I believe you remember." He cocked his head, and his eyes twinkled as if he could read her thoughts. "My heart danced with joy, but then, you were gone that quick." He snapped his fingers to demonstrate.

How one man's will could carry her across time, even for a second, was a mystery. The idea of being out of control should have frightened her, but paradoxically it didn't. Clayton didn't frighten her.

"I have no say in this?" She placed her fisted hands on her hips and threw him a glance that had the more friendly interns backing away.

"Ah, my Nora, the same fire as before." He shook his head at his words and then added, "I do not claim to understand the ins and outs of such matters. Your will enters into it, too. At first, you didn't stay long. I think I surprised you. Now, your stay has been much longer than before. It must mean you want to be here."

His confident smile and knowing look irritated Nora. She thought of a few put-downs that worked well on other men who tried to chat her up, but a log fell in the fire, sending up a flurry of sparks. The sudden motion stopped her automatic response and drew her attention to the sparks as they flared and disappeared.

Her glaze went back to Clayton, whose alert countenance was brighter than any spark. What if he was right? How could that be? She'd never had the opportunity to have a normal boyfriend as most teen girls did. It didn't mean she hadn't had a few crushes. Still, they paled in comparison to what she felt sitting there, a sense almost of belonging. It was hard to understand why this one man would have such an effect on her, especially after she'd given up on that part of her life. Still, it wasn't fair to this charming man to let him believe that there might be something between them.

She stood, unaware of how to explain what she needed to say, but it couldn't be explained sitting. Hands behind her back, she paced around the fire, one side of her body alternately heated by the closeness to the fire while the other side felt the nip of the falling temperatures. "Clayton, you seem like a nice man."

"Ah, here it comes." He raised his hand toward the sky. "Just like when you were a princess and I a lowly footman. You gave me the long speech about how different our stations were in life."

"I did?" Nora almost remembered, if she really tried, a haughty princess and a lowly footman in some dark corner of her memory.

"Do you remember now?" Clayton stood and watched her as she paced. "Do you remember how I responded?"

Memories of the offended footman sweeping up the haughty princess materialized in her mind. "You, you, you..." She was unsure how to say it. "You changed my mind."

"That I did. That was then. I understand things are different now, and you need healing more than a lusty embrace." He walked slowly toward her, stopped a foot from her, and held out his arms. "I am here for you."

A cry bubbled up in her throat as she took two running steps into his open arms. Clayton wrapped his arms around her and rocked her gently. "Go ahead, cry it out. You have the right."

The crying she'd denied herself for so many years suddenly erupted, flowing like lava. Nora wept until she could weep no more. Her sobs continued for minutes until they became less and less, morphing into occasional hiccupping.

The wood smoke irritated her eyes as she lifted her head from Clayton's shirt and vest. "I'm sorry. I don't know what got into me."

His embrace tightened as he rested his head on top of hers. "You needed the cry. I am willing to bet you do not allow yourself to cry or show any weakness often."

With an indelicate sniff, Nora wiped her nose with the back of her hand. "You'd be right. I can't remember the last time I cried. I suspect it was when my dog Brownie was killed when I was twelve."

Clayton gave her an extra squeeze before loosening the embrace.

Cold, she wanted to ask him why he let go, but realized he was fading away. "Clayton."

Chapter Four

Nora tossed and turned in her sleep, aware on some level that she was searching for Clayton. No matter where she went in her dreams, she could not find him. Her alarm sounded, pulling her out of a troubled sleep, one of the few times she welcomed morning, even as early as it was. To continue to sleep and traverse the dream world in search of Clayton would only equal heartache. Might as well get up and study for her test. She stumbled out of bed and headed for the kitchen.

Carrying two slices of toast liberally coated with peanut butter, she sat down at the battered table and began to peruse the infectious diseases chapter as she consumed her breakfast.

Her fingers brushed the names carved into the table. She and Tonya had rescued the relic from the trash. Students moved out all the time, even tossing appliances away to avoid the trouble of carrying them home or perhaps hoping for a new style the upcoming year. Most of those students had parents who bought them everything they needed or wanted. Half the items tossed were usable, but still ended up in a dumpster. Finances forced Nora to be much less discriminating.

Between the diner and a food budget, including a steady diet of peanut butter and bread, she made the most of every penny she could. Good grades in high school had landed her a merit scholarship that paid most of her tuition. The goal of having a real job that didn't involve chopping onions and having an actual car kept her focused.

Both she and Tonya had contemplated living together after school, since neither one had any plans otherwise, but suddenly those simple dreams were no longer enough.

Taking another bite of toast, she chewed contemplatively. What was wrong with her goals? They served her through four years of college and a lackluster relationship with Ogden.

Dusting the crumbs off her fingers, she turned another page in her textbook. Many of the students had switched to electronic books, alleviating the need to carry around twenty-pound monstrosities that caused her to bend under the weight, rather like a mountain climber. Still, the old paper textbooks crowded the shelves at the nearby thrift store. She'd even plucked a few from the dumpster. Half the students who dropped out had started in medical school.

Being financially independent used to be enough for her. Having a job where she helped others was her ultimate goal. It was all still good, but she wanted more. Why couldn't she have the feeling of belonging and comfort she'd felt in Clayton's arms? Why did all her goals have to be so damn practical? Wasn't love part of the fabric of her life?

Somehow, she'd suppressed part of her upbringing. Her determination in obtaining her nurse practitioner's degree demonstrated her belief that she could do anything if she imagined it and worked for it. While accepting that hard work paid off, she'd brushed aside the belief that one day she could fall madly, hopelessly in love. More important, she didn't believe anyone could feel that way about her.

No wonder she'd accepted her role as unpaid assistant in Ogden's life. Maybe playing the part of a human service animal was as good as she was going to get. Her stomach clenched and rolled at the thought, making her a little nauseated. Plenty of people fell in and out of love several times. The residents of the surrounding apartments demonstrated that fairly well. Tonya stayed guarded in her affections, never allowing herself to fall headfirst, regarding the man as empty of actual value, rather like a dessert drink.

In the end, Tonya did partake, while Nora settled for a man who stirred none of her emotions.

Her fingers traveled the printed pages while she read the text aloud, hoping to imprint it on her memory. How could she study when her life spiraled out of control?

The sound of Tonya's alarm clock meant her roommate would be up soon. As much as Nora longed to talk to someone, she didn't dare. What could she say? Some dream man was making her doubt everything she thought was real, even though, unlike most people, she'd had real experience with the unusual in seeing her sister transported through time.

Only a few years ago, Leah had found herself in a past century, battling people who wanted to put her to death while she worked to correct a wrong assumption. Nana had called in all her coven friends, and Nora had gone home to do the protection magic that may have saved her little sister. She knew for sure her little sister had gone back in time—as had her grandfather.

That would mean she could, too.

How could she determine if her dreams were time travel or perhaps a form of astral projection, which allowed her spirit to travel by leaving her body? While she'd heard of people, especially monks, being able to do that, she'd never personally known anyone who could. Was there something she could do to determine the validity of the experience? Should she ask Tonya to check in on her to see if her body still lay under the covers late at night? She'd hate to put her friend to all that trouble. It could be embarrassing, too.

Tonya walked into the room, yawning, and headed for the coffeepot. Some low-level grumbling reminded Nora she'd drunk the entire pot and forgotten to start a new one. Caffeine was probably the only dietary vice her roommate allowed herself.

"Sorry, roomie." She winced as she said the words. It was not a good time to have memory problems or hear voices. Was there ever a good time?

The smell of coffee drifted through the room. Tonya carried in two cups. Setting one beside Nora's textbook, she pulled out the other chair. "What's going on with you?"

Nora dropped the highlighter she'd been using to underline keywords, a trick to commit them to long-term memory. "What makes you think anything is wrong?"

Tonya took a sip of coffee and rolled her eyes appreciatively. "We've known each other for almost four years. I am willing to bet I know you better than your family."

Nora reached for her cup to delay answering. The first sip of the bitter brew had her wrinkling her nose. Even though she preferred sugar and plenty of it, Tonya called it the white death, which meant it seldom made it into the apartment, except for the few packets Nora smuggled home from the diner. She swallowed the dark liquid, appreciating the kick if not the flavor. Her stomach gurgled in response, since it was her fourth cup. Setting her cup down, she looked at Tonya, who appeared surprisingly alert for having just awakened.

"I've had trouble sleeping."

Tonya nodded. "That I noticed. Why?"

Biting her bottom lip, she considered how much to confess.

Tonya shook her head. "Out with it, girl. I can see you deciding how much to tell me."

"A person would think you were a mind reader." The fact her roommate could read her so well was disconcerting.

Tonya winked. "Nope, you're so OCD about everything that when you vary from your usual routines and start forgetting things, I know something is up."

Finishing her toast, Nora licked her fingers. "What did I do that made you think something was up?"

Her roommate laughed briefly. "What didn't you do? For almost five days, I haven't seen any lists anywhere with those black, finished slashes through the various items. One day, you forgot your watch."

Forgot her watch, she did remember that. It was as bad as most people forgetting their phone. Her hand slipped up to her neck and rubbed. The tension from the night before began to return. "I am a little worried myself. It seems like everything I planned for my life is wrong."

Tonya placed both palms on the table and leaned forward. "Medicine is your life. You're good at it. You don't want to do it anymore?"

Her roommate's words only added to her muddled state. "I didn't say that. I do want to be in the medical field in some form. It's just that the life I planned out for myself"—she threw her hands in the air over the futility of explaining something she didn't fully understand—"doesn't seem to fit anymore."

Tonya placed her index finger against her temple as she gave that some thought. "If you mean Ogden, I'd say he never fit. What are you going to do about him?"

Part of it was Ogden. Her roommate's casual reply helped her solidify part of her problem. "As for Ogden, I guess I am already doing it. I am making myself unavailable to run his little errands."

"About time." Tonya's accompanying snort relayed her feelings about the opportunistic Ogden. "That man saw you coming. He read you well. Have to give him credit there. Most of the nurses would have told him what he could do with himself. I imagine more than a few did."

The picture Tonya painted was not a pretty one. Nora had hesitated to let her roommate know she was keeping company with the fussy doctor because she'd seen through him in a heartbeat. Unfortunately, the picture said more about her than she wanted to acknowledge. "You're right. I heard rumors, but I thought a man, any man, would keep other men at a distance."

Tonya knocked on the table in her mirth. "I am scaring away all the spirits who might carry news of your ignorance. Girl, men hit on women, especially young, hot women like yourself." She put her hand up to stop Nora's reply. "Go ahead and tell me you cut off your hair to be less attractive, how you wear your uniforms loose to disguise your curves. It's not working. Your Ice Queen act only draws the players closer. All you managed to do is discourage the decent, shy men. The users know your scent."

"Damn, those were the ones I hoped to discourage." Nora scowled. Her roomie's words had a ring of truth that didn't please her at all. "Yesterday Ogden tried to flag me down when I left the hospital. Instead of acknowledging him, I got on the elevator with all the other students."

"Burned his butt good, but his type won't go away easily. Continue to make yourself unavailable. Men do this all the time. They quit coming around until you realize you haven't seen them for weeks when you see them out with some other woman." Tonya rocked back on the hind legs of the chair.

"I can do that without too much work," Nora admitted, slowly abandoning her plan to continue to see Ogden until she graduated. No doubt, Ogden used her, but she was just as guilty of using him. Strangely, seeing Ogden would feel too much like cheating on Clayton. This should have been the final sign she was losing it, fear of upsetting the boyfriend who existed only in her dreams.

A glance at her watch propelled her up. "I am late again. How did that happen?" She flew into the bathroom to brush her teeth, while Tonya trailed behind.

Tonya stood in the doorway of the bathroom, sharing her thoughts. "This is what I mean. You're never late. You're usually at the bus stop ten minutes before the bus. If I didn't know better, I'd think you were crushing on some guy."

Nora looked in the mirror as she brushed her teeth. Tonya's image hovered over her left shoulder. *Crushing on some guy? How ridiculous is that, especially, if I told her it was my imaginary friend?* Clayton's image formed behind her right shoulder. Her head whipped around so fast she dribbled toothpaste on her uniform. Her heart rate slowed when she realized only her friend stood behind her, wearing a concerned expression.

Nora tried to smile around the toothbrush. Spitting, she wiped her mouth on a hand towel and headed for the door. Tonya stepped out of the way at the last minute. Her friend followed her to her room, where Nora grabbed her packed backpack. Yesterday's soiled uniform lay on the floor with her abandoned pajamas. She picked up the pajamas and sniffed. Wood smoke.

"See that." Tonya gestured at the clothes. "You never leave your clothes on the floor. Now, you're sniffing them like a frat boy trying to find something clean to wear."

Her roommate's words registered as she considered the implications of her wood-smoke-scented jammies. She wanted to sniff them again to be sure, but she hadn't the time. "Don't do my laundry while I am gone."

Her unexpected pronouncement had Tonya balling her fists on her hips and opening her mouth in surprise. She sputtered before Nora got out the door, "When have I ever done your laundry?"

"Never." Nora shouldered her bag on and located her bus pass for the sprint to the stop.

Tonya followed to the landing and yelled after her as she took the stairs two at a time, "What's wrong with you?"

Nora wondered that herself. Her roommate's shouting attracted the attention of other neighbors. Great, now everyone would wonder about her.

The man across the hall ran down the stairs in tandem with her to catch the bus. He assumed she and Tonya were lovers, since he shared his apartment with his guy pal.

"Problems in paradise?" he queried.

Nora just grimaced. It would be too hard to explain. Besides, the man would accuse her again of not having the courage to come out of the closet. The rumble of the bus turning the corner caused her to break into a jog with her neighbor following.

On the bus, she made her way to the back, where the wannabe tough guys and sometimes crazies sat, such as women bundled up in several sweaters even when the temps were in the triple digits and men who had aluminum foil wrapped around their ball caps to prevent aliens from reading their thoughts. With her imaginary friend, she'd fit right in. Of course, her neighbor wouldn't follow, because the crazies freaked him out. It would give her time to think, as opposed to fending off helpful advice from her earnest neighbor. .

Wood smoke. How could that have happened? If her jammies smelled like onions, she'd blame that on the diner. The smell of onions and grease soaked into her pores, flavoring her skin and scenting her hair. A survey once proved that men were attracted to the smell of cooking meat as opposed to the most expensive perfumes. Maybe that's what made her attractive to the opposite sex, as opposed to gorgeous eyes or a shapely torso. The siren call of frying hamburger probably netted her the creepy admirer at the diner. Still, it didn't answer the wood-smoke question.

If she'd had time, she'd have sniffed the pajamas to ascertain for sure whether the smell was there or imagined. Maybe she could get a whiff of rabbit stew, or better yet, a trace of Clayton would be nice. His arms around her had been warm and comforting, but his scent had reminded her of something spicy, though nothing close to current colognes. She smiled at the thought.

"Whoever you're thinking about must be handsome, right?" a woman bundled in several sweaters inquired with a nudge of her elbow.

Nora turned to look at the woman rather than trying to ignore her. Her sweaters were all complementary shades and layered a way that seemed intentional. "Yes, yes, I am," she answered, not bothering to deny it. How had this woman ended up riding around in the bus endlessly? Although, Nora couldn't be sure the woman rode without a destination. "Are you on your way to work?"

"Goodness, no. I retired some years ago. Used to work in a meat warehouse. Almost thirty years working in a thirty-degree storage facility. Thought when I got out of there, I'd be warm finally. Didn't happen. The cold sank into my bones. Most people probably think I'm crazy always wearing sweaters."

Nora hurried to deny she'd ever had such thoughts.

The elderly woman gave her a broad smile. "Don't worry about it. You are one of the few to ever sit beside me on purpose."

The woman's willingness to think the best of her made her feel about two inches tall. It also showed that if you took the time to really listen to people, instead of making assumptions, you'd find out a lot more. She'd have to remember that, since it would be helpful in her practice.

Her hospital came into view, causing Nora to pick up her pack. "See ya," she said, nodding in the woman's direction and standing to make her way to the door.

The woman waved and added, "Hold on to a man who makes you smile."

Nora turned to wave once her feet hit the pavement and found Allen, her neighbor, regarding her in confusion through the bus windows. Difficult to believe it took a woman he probably regarded as crazy to finally convince him that she wasn't a lesbian.

Perhaps she should listen to the woman and hang on to Clayton. She wished she knew how. The fact she no longer heard his voice worried her. Could she somehow be losing contact with him?

Not hardly, sweetheart. I chose not to talk to you since it appeared I distressed you too much.

Her anxiety melted away with the sound of his soothing lilt. Her first reaction was to answer him with actual words, but she checked herself before she did. She thought the words: *You're back.*

I never left you, but often I can't talk to you. If I could have my way, I'd be with you every second of every day, but that would be selfish of me. Could be that's not what you want?

Nora entered the hospital, distracted by the sound of Clayton's voice. She answered the friendly guard's greeting as she drifted toward the elevator bank. The sound of a familiar voice broke through her absorption enough for her to make a break for the women's bathroom. *Great. Ogden.* It seemed the more she tried to ignore him, the more he seemed to appear. If he'd spotted her, then he'd wait right outside the door. If only, there was another way out.

The sound of lockers slamming reminded her that she was in the restroom adjacent to the female staff's locker room. One of the older nurses came up behind her.

"Who are you hiding from, sweetie?"

"Ogden Graves, Doctor." She bit her lips when she realized her mistake. The woman could march out there and tell Ogden she was inside.

Instead, the woman shook her head and guided Nora away from the door.

"Pompous ass. You do good to hide from him. He thinks women are on this earth to serve men. Heard he even has one nursing student dedicated to do his bidding. I'm not sure what he has on her to get her to run his errands. He's nothing to look at and is definitely a zero in the charm department." She gestured at the door to the locker room. "Go through there and use the other door. It opens up into the nurses' lounge. You can slip through there into the next hallway outside of the pediatric offices."

"Thanks. You're a lifesaver. I've never been in the nurses' lounge, being a student and all." She made a break for the door to escape before someone named her as Ogden's errand girl. People at the hospital didn't think for a moment that there was anything romantic between them. Instead, they believed he had some dirt on her to keep her running and fetching.

For a change, she didn't doubt her attractiveness, but wondered if Ogden played off their relationship to keep his options open. It sounded like him. With this exalted opinion of himself, he would assume he could do better. The fact he thought she was beneath him made her angry. Still, hadn't she accepted it all along. This wasn't anything new. Suddenly, the idea was repulsive. No more running and fetching for the grand and glorious Dr. Graves and she doubted anyone would replace her.

Her plan to fade out of Ogden's orbit was a cowardly one. Still, it wouldn't do any good to make a stand. He'd only ignore it. He'd blame it on hormones and assign her another errand.

Clayton's voice sounded inside her head, making her smile: *I would never let you go if you were mine.*

The resident from the other day came into view. She'd forgotten his name. All she remembered was he was friendly.

The man smiled at her, and his eyes lit up as they met hers. "That's what I like to see, a beautiful smile. Dare I hope that smile is for me?"

Scalawag.

Clayton's growled comment rattled her. She wasn't sure if she could handle a voice in her head and a conversation at the same time.

I will go.

A feeling of loss replaced his voice.

The young doctor still smiled at her. She wasn't sure what he'd asked her, but he expected an answer. She decided to go with something indefinite. "Possibly." Unaware of what she was being indefinite about, she watched the man grow even more animated.

"Great, great, I was hoping my excellent bedside manner would wear you down eventually." He fell in step with her.

"Um." Great, now look what she'd done. A quick glance at his nametag identified him as T. Mangano. "Dr. Mangano, I think there's been a misunderstanding." Her stride lengthened as she saw the red light above the elevator bank, indicating a car on the way.

The man looked perplexed, and his smile lessened a bit. "It's Terrence. You really don't remember me."

Actually, she did, but not in the I-was-thinking-of-you-fondly way. It was better to admit she hadn't thought of him at all. "Um, no."

"I am so sorry I bothered you." He walked briskly away.

He might have been one of the nice ones Tonya had mentioned. Life was easier when she didn't interact with other people, though she wasn't sure she could get through life not interacting. Of course, it was also easier when she didn't have an additional voice in her head.

Hey, I heard that.

Nora stepped onto the elevator and worked her way to the back, making sure not to smile in reaction to Clayton's words. There was no reason to give someone else the wrong message.

Chapter Five

Clinical was finally over and past lunchtime for most. Several students rushed for the elevator as the doors slid open. Nora moved back to allow others to enter. A woman jostled her arm and grinned at her before speaking.

"I saw what you did back there." She moved her eyebrows up and down rapidly, like a cartoon character.

"Um." Nora hesitated, trying to recall the female's name. It was something with a T. Tess, Trish, Tory. She tried out the names in her head. She threw an apologetic smile at the petite brunette.

The woman leaned closer and raised up on tiptoes enough to whisper in Nora's ear. "It's Tricia."

Of course, she would have gotten to that name eventually. "Yes, yes, I remember. You're the one who didn't like dissecting the cats in anatomy class."

Tricia grimaced about the same time the elevator doors slid open. They all shuffled forward into the lobby. "I will forever be remembered as Cat Girl. There's a story behind it, though. I lost my cat when I was a kid, and my loving, older brother told me it was picked up by cat bundlers who caught cats for medical research." She sighed a little and pointed to the outside doors.

Nora nodded and fell into step with her. Good chance they were both heading to the same place. *Yay.* "You heading to the university?"

"You know it, for the wonderful epidemic exam." The sneer in her voice allowed any eavesdroppers to be well aware of her feelings about the upcoming test. "You drive?"

"I wish." Nora slid her hand into her pocket to retrieve her bus pass and looked into the direction of the crowded bus stop. Sweet Goddess, how she hated balancing herself against the bus's motion while maintaining a death grip on the rubber strap that time of day. Plenty of jerks used it as an opportunity to cop a feel as they squeezed by. The first time she'd almost flashed back to that night so long ago. Now she settled for hissing, "Jerk," which usually made them chuckle. The last two times she'd taken advantage of her long feet by turning one slightly to trip the creeps.

"Would you like a ride?" Tricia offered. "You could quiz me about the test, since you're such a brainiac."

Nora started to protest the brainiac label but focused on another word instead. Ride. Tricia had offered her a ride. "Yes."

Would she rather sit in a seat and not be subject to pawing as she hung from a strap? That was a no-brainer. "I'd love a ride and would be willing to quiz you."

Tricia pointed to the right parking lot before she started walking. "I could use your help, but what I really want to know is how you got the sexy Dr. Mangano to follow you around."

True, he'd talked to her, but it wasn't something she'd wanted. "I'm not sure that I did anything." Her eyes traveled over the sea of parked cars. Instead of following the road, her companion created a crooked path by squeezing past expensive sedans. Obviously, they were in the physicians' parking lot. The pricey vehicles gave way to minivans and older vehicles, which meant they'd entered staff parking.

Tricia grumbled more to herself, but her words still carried. "Damn, I hate it when my mother is right. That's what she told me. The men always go after the ones who play hard to get."

Nora followed until they stopped at a battered-looking compact. Tricia unlocked it with a squeeze of her key fob. Her new friend opened the passenger door and swept the untidy piles of books and papers into the back seat.

"Sorry, I wasn't expecting company." Tricia grinned as she gave the last book a toss into the back.

Nora tried not to wince. She treated her books extremely well because she hoped to resell the majority of them. A few she might keep as reference, but constant medical advances made textbooks dated in a matter of months. "Don't worry about it. I'm glad for the ride. You have no idea how much I appreciate it."

Tricia started the car and pulled out into the slow-moving traffic before Nora began the questions. "What do you know about cholera?"

Tricia lowered her window, letting in a whiff of diesel-fuel-tainted air. "I know enough to know I don't want to get it. Seriously, it causes diarrhea, vomiting, and dehydration. People used to die from it awhile back."

Nora's muscles clinched as Tricia guided the small car across several lanes without signaling. It was better than the bus. Of course, on the bus she never paid attention to the driving because she was too busy either studying or, most often, collapsed in an exhausted heap. Inhaling, she tried to recover her train of thought. "How do people get cholera?"

The small car zoomed into a minuscule spot between two hulking SUVs, causing the driver of one to honk and swear.

Tricia answered the enraged driver with a flip of her finger, which resulted in more honking. "Hmm, is that the one that was spread by fleas on rats? No, wait. That was the bubonic plague. You got me. What is it?"

Nora's fingers lingered near her neck. Would it be rude to check her pulse? Probably. Besides, she knew it would be high. Her hand dropped back to her lap. "Cholera results from contaminated water and food. The bacteria are present in feces. People experiencing natural disasters, living in crowded, unsanitary conditions such as refugee camps are prone to contracting it as well. There have been cases of people getting it from seafood pulled from the Gulf of Mexico."

"Gives a whole new meaning to bad clams, huh?" Tricia giggled at her joke. "We haven't had much of a problem with it here in the United States, have we?"

Nora's eyes cut to Tricia as she drove without a care. The woman was right: She did need to study if her last question was any indication. "Well, actually, it was a problem until about 1870. People didn't really understand about sanitation and clean water. Their outhouses were often near water sources. If that wasn't bad enough, the domesticated animals crapped in the water, too. All they knew was the water made them sick. So, they stuck to a diet of ale and milk. The fermentation killed the bacteria in the water."

Tricia laughed as she turned into the university parking lot. "Those were the days. Ale for breakfast. Beer for lunch."

Nora stifled the desire to point out they probably had milk for breakfast. "Luckily, the germ theory caught on, which in itself is amazing, since most people discounted Van Leeuwenhoek's microorganisms work. They chose to contribute illness to punishment for sins."

Tricia spotted another student pulling out and immediately punched the accelerator, cutting off a slow-moving pickup. She maneuvered the small car into the space before shifting into park and twisting off the ignition.

"That was lucky," Nora said, not knowing what else to say to her kamikaze-driver friend.

"Oh, no," Tricia said, opening the car door. "Not lucky. You have to make your own luck, which is what I do. I saw you in the elevator. Everyone knows your smart, and I knew I wasn't ready for the test. I should at least recognize cholera, probably the bubonic plague, and influenza, right? Think smallpox, too."

Nora opened her car door, unsure how to reply to that remark. While the woman freely admitted her machinations to use Nora for information, she'd used Tricia for transportation, even if the ride had taken a few years off her life.

They walked toward the life science building without talking while a few late students sprinted past them. The smell of cut grass rode the breeze as a grounds maintenance employee buzzed across the green expanse on his oversized lawn mower.

Make your own luck.

The words stuck in her mind. It sounded like something her nana might say. Working almost sixteen hours a day, she'd pushed herself through college. No luck, just plain hard work, but luck would have been so much easier. Her father's voice echoed in her mind, reminding her that nothing was free. It didn't stop her from asking, "How do you make your own luck?"

Tricia's eyes sparkled before she replied, making her look a bit like Hollywood's stereotype of an elf or even a sprite. "You have to have opportunities. Lots of them." She abruptly threw her free arm out to gesture.

Nora jerked to a stop to avoid the arm. Opportunities, she understood that. "Okay, how will I find all these opportunities?"

"Looks to me like you've already found some on your own." Tricia smirked a little and waved at a male student passing them, several books clutched to his chest as he walked with a determined line to his lips. "Hi, Todd."

The student looked up. His eyes blinked a few times behind his thick glasses, before he located the source of the greeting. A smile tugged at his lips, making him almost attractive. "Hi, Tricia."

"Working hard, I see." Tricia angled her head toward the books. "It's no wonder you are setting the curve for the rest of us."

Nora watched a slight blush work its way up Todd's neck, but his smile grew along with it.

He tried to brush aside the obvious compliment. "Most of the professors no longer grade on the curve. They use a rubric."

"Really?" Tricia exclaimed with enough enthusiasm that suggested the nervous Todd had imparted the true meaning of life.

Nora looked at her watch. She didn't have time to watch the byplay of medical students in their natural habitat. Dr. Lansky, the instructor, would lock the door against any late arrivals. Her actions were against school policy, but by the time a person got any results from a lodged complaint, he or she would already have flunked out of infectious diseases and would be almost a year behind in the program. Besides, who would want to take the class again from a hostile Dr. Lansky?

With this in mind, Nora elbowed her friend. "We're going to be late."

"Okay," Tricia said. "See ya later, Todd." She held up one hand to the student, who acknowledged her with a head bob since his arms were full.

Nora's long strides made her new friend work to keep pace with her. Aware of Tricia jogging to keep up, she murmured, "Sorry," but did not slow.

Tricia kept up her combination jog-walk and even talked. "Todd is an opportunity. He's a braniac like you and helped me through chemistry. I'm not sure why nurses even have to take chemistry. It isn't like we're going to develop new drugs, only administer them."

"Don't you feel like you're using him?" The words slipped out of Nora's mouth before she could consider how insulting they might sound. Once out, she longed to retract them. The open double doors of the lecture hall loomed ahead. If she could just reach them, it would be a form of sanctuary. She doubted Tricia would ever want to talk to her again.

The tinkle of her companion's laugh surprised her into stopping. "You aren't mad at me?"

"No, of course not. How can I be mad at a person who actually says what she thinks?" She turned to wink at Nora, and they both continued walking. "All human interaction is give-and-take. I talked to Todd, and he's pleased. Other students see him talking to not one, but two beautiful women, and his value goes up in the eyes of both males and females."

It made sense. Instead of just taking from other people, as Nora had originally assumed, Tricia was bartering. It may have been an unspoken agreement. She wanted to ask more about creating luck, but Dr. Lansky's white-coated figured appeared near the open lecture hall doors.

"Run." Nora yelped the word and suited her actions to it.

Both she and Tricia made it inside before the instructor slapped the doors shut and locked them. She turned and gave them both a measuring look, then walked to the podium.

Nora grinned at her companion, and then located an empty seat. Grumbling and some cursing slipped through the locked doors. Not all students took Dr. Lansky's reputation seriously. A few expected college to be like high school, where their parents or a kind counselor ran interference. Rules didn't apply to them. Not only did they soon discover the opposite, but also that there were myriad expectations from various instructors.

The smack of a blue book caught her attention as it hit the desk surface. Most professors used the testing center for examinations. The students logged in on the network computers and took the usual multiple-choices exams. Not Dr. Lansky. She believed students were able to circumvent the testing center's safeguards and cheated.

Nora knew they did, from getting information from students who'd taken previous tests to sending other students to take their tests for them. Since fellow students manned the testing center, it was easy to persuade them to look the other way. Often, they never knew, since the test-taker might use someone else's login.

That would explain Dr. Lansky's diligence in monitoring her own exams. If that wasn't enough, the tests were in essay form. The woman believed those in the medical field should not only be able to put their thoughts down on paper, but it should be legible. Everyone knew doctors and nurses typed everything now. Still, it did spoil the plans of any would-be cheaters.

A glance at the board revealed their prompt, written in Dr. Lansky's perfect cursive of unusually straight lines. How she managed that baffled Nora. She pondered the prompt as she rolled the sharpened pencil between her fingers. Most students wrote in pen, but her confidence wasn't that high.

You enter a village in the late-eighteenth century. The residents are showing a lack of energy. Few are abed with diarrhea, while others complain of fever and show symptoms of a rash. What is it? How would you treat it?

Nora sneaked a glance at Tricia, whose mouth was open. Good, Nora wasn't the only one baffled. It could be a number of illnesses. It could be typhoid fever or cholera. It could also be influenza or even food poisoning. Exhaling a long breath, she watched Dr. Lansky slowly pace the aisles, having to squeeze past the students. Other students were writing as if they knew. Why didn't she?

Biting her bottom lip, Nora considered that most epidemics started with poor sanitation and crowded conditions. Epidemics usually started in cities. With that in mind, if a high standard of sanitation was implemented, and the sick individuals were quarantined, the illness might be controlled. There wouldn't be any antibiotics available, because penicillin hadn't been invented yet.

Nora gnawed on the pencil, trying to think of a way to relieve the people's symptoms with what they had in their time. Herbal tea, that's it. Nana tended to dose their family with tea, depending on their symptoms. Nausea or upset stomach merited peppermint tea, while fennel was useful for those with the runs. Unfortunately, Nana usually withheld it for a few hours, declaring the body was trying to rid itself of the toxin. Now, she knew what to do, but she didn't know what she was dealing with.

Go with what you do know. She tried to reassure herself as she carefully printed all the illnesses that shared the symptoms and were common to that century. Her sanitation precautions, boiling all water and washing all clothing and linens in hot soapy water, might have been a hard sell in that period, but it was doable. One of her professors had mentioned that more people died during the Civil War from surgeons with dirty hands and dysentery than gunshot.

The other students left in spurts, interrupting her flow of thoughts as they clumped out of the room. With each group, Nora experienced a nervous twinge. What if she wasn't done in time? A few more students pushed past her seat. Tricia touched her shoulder and mouthed the word, "Bye." Nora nodded slightly, careful to avoid the appearance of cheating.

A quick look confirmed her fear that she was the last student in the room. Why did she make things so hard? Why didn't she breeze through like the others or even resort to an ink pen? Sighing, she realized she was who she was. A methodical worker and analytical thinker, which meant she never did anything quickly.

Well, she could cook fast. However, she never did anything speedy that required actual thought.

Holding up the blue book, she carefully read each page, checking for missing or misspelled words. Finally, she forced herself to stand and walk to the front table, where all the blue books sat caged in a wire box. Dr. Lansky sat at the table, reading an exam with an uncapped red marker. Occasionally snorting with mirth, she circled a section and wrote a remark. Well, at least Nora knew it wasn't her exam.

Her grip tightened on her blue book as she drew closer.

Dr. Lansky looked up. "Nora Carpenter, I would be interested in your opinion of my prompt." The woman lifted her eyebrows a tiny bit.

"I found it to be a difficult prompt since many illnesses show the same symptoms. You also did not identify the location of the village, which in turn would give me a hint about the ethnic makeup of the population. Two important things I didn't know if good sanitation was in place at that time and if the illnesses would spread through contact, water, food, touch, and possibly the air. So, I was unsure how to treat and label the illness."

Whoa, what if Dr. Lansky hadn't really wanted her opinion? What if she'd just shot herself in the foot? After all, her test had yet to receive a grade. Would Dr. Lansky be willing to forget her pithy little speech?

Nora watched as her instructor capped the red pen and laid it aside. She pushed up from her seated position to stand facing Nora. "Were you frustrated that you didn't know immediately what was wrong with the residents of the mythical village?"

Nora had felt some frustration but had contributed it to fouling up her perfect 4.0 GPA. "I did feel a high level of frustration."

Dr. Lansky smiled, which to some would only have validated her reputation as being ruthless, but Nora didn't consider it a mean smile. There had been more to the question than a simple epidemic.

Nora asked, "Were you trying to show us how doctors in the eighteenth century were clueless about what they might be treating?"

The doctor nodded. "That's part of it, but even in this century, with all our special tests and equipment, medicine requires observation and experimentation. Physicians willing to go with the quick or popular answer can end up killing their patient. They'll explain it away in other ways, but it amounts to the same."

It was a sobering thought. As a physician assistant, she'd be making some of those calls on her own. It would pay to watch and listen very closely. "Part of good practice is listening to the patient?" Nora asked, already knowing the answer.

Dr. Lansky started to agree, but stopped. "It is more than that. Sometimes it is getting the patient to talk. Other times, it's seeing through the words to understand what they aren't saying, and other times, it is asking the right questions. Unfortunately, we don't have any classes for those skills, but I believe you have them."

"Me?" Nora squeaked the word, much to her embarrassment. She pointed to herself, foolishly since no one else was in the room.

"Yes, you." Dr. Lansky punctuated her answer with an emphatic head bob. "You are my best student. Probably the best in the program. I would love to see you as a doctor as opposed to an assistant. With your level of ability right now, we could put you in the eighteenth century, and you'd save hundreds of lives, maybe even thousands."

Nora rested her hand against the table. Her legs felt a little weak. Could be shock. She'd never expected one of the toughest instructors in the program to heap praise on her.

"Thank you," she murmured the words as she held out her blue book.

The woman took the book and tucked it under the other ones. "Your exam will be my reward after getting through all the other tests. I had every diagnosis, from chicken pox to the plague, but not one student suggested that he or she didn't know what the illness was. It takes real character to admit when you don't know. Be glad you have that character."

Nora tried for a smile, but was unsure if her lips tilted up appropriately. All she wanted to do was drop her mouth open in absolute amazement. Here was a woman who'd never cracked a smile the entire semester, and she was grinning at her as if Nora had done something great.

Covering her mouth, she coughed before she could say anything. Clearing her throat, she managed to croak out the words, "I appreciate your comments more than you can possibly know."

The other woman's brow furrowed briefly. "Maybe. I might have a clue. I was once a student like you, but at that time, they did not consider females as doctor candidates, medical or otherwise."

As wonderful as the conversation was, Nora felt awkward and longed to escape back to the life she knew. "I see you proved them wrong."

Dr. Lansky folded her arms and looked supremely pleased with herself. "I did, didn't I? Don't let me make you late to your next class."

Nora made eye contact before dashing out the door. Was she being rude? She yelled back into the lecture hall, "See ya."

As she half-jogged to reach the bus stop, her remark replayed in her brain. Real stupid to say, "See ya" to one of the most-feared lecturers on staff.

The rumble of the bus along with a healthy belch of diesel fumes alerted her that her ride had arrived. Palming her pass, she hustled into line with the other passengers. It wouldn't do for her to be late to work. It wasn't as if she'd be fired, but the thought of inconveniencing her co-workers bothered her. Her lateness put her at the end of the line as the people in front of her grabbed the empty seats.

Damn. She wanted to rest before she started her shift. She scoured the area, hoping for an overlooked seat. There was one in the back, right between an earbud-plugged teen and a sleeping woman whose lips trembled with each snore. Not ideal, but it would allow her to gobble her mid-morning snack, which she had yet to consume. Her stomach gave a minor growl as if agreeing. Her feet were headed in that direction when she felt someone behind her. A glance over her right shoulder revealed a confused, elderly woman desperately searching for a seat. Nora sighed, moved aside, and pointed the seat out to the woman.

"Oh, thank you, dear," the woman said, as she made her unsteady way to the back of the bus.

Nora reached for the overhead strap. "No problem, ma'am."

Her stomach emitted another growl. Someone was bound to get off before the bus reached the diner, allowing her to sit and choke down her granola bar. It didn't make sense to eat before her late lunch, but standing on her feet for four hours of clinical plus another hour in class took a tremendous amount of energy. Twisting her arm on the strap to see her watch indicated she didn't even have time to sit down at the counter and order. At least, she could eat something in the kitchen.

This small possibility lightened her mood. Why should she be gloomy? Dr. Lansky had told her she'd make a good doctor. She'd be willing to bet the good doctor seldom shared those words with many. More likely, she shared the opposite observation.

Her mind drifted into a stupor in which she was aware of the bus moving and its location, but little else.

So why aren't you going to be a doctor? You would be a good one.

Clayton's voice in her head caused her to stumble forward, but at least she still had hold of the strap to prevent falling. By this time, you'd think she'd be used to Clayton's voice. Well, at least she recognized it. Mental illness took many forms, she reminded herself. One out of four people had some type. The statistics, however, did nothing to reassure her.

I am not a mental illness. You are not crazy. It actually takes a great deal of work on my part to contact you. I would like it if you'd show a little more appreciation.

Sorry. Her face crinkled into an apologetic grin, making the man in a fast-food smock and seated just under her arm regard her strangely then look away.

Why aren't you studying to be a doctor?

Clayton's question echoed Dr. Lansky's remarks. Apparently, the man could read her thoughts. She tried to shape them so they made sense. *I never really considered being a doctor, ever. School is expensive. I got some scholarships. My parents scraped together a little bit of money to help. I saved that, though. I work at the diner to pay for my rent, food, and utilities. I'm in my fifth year of schooling, too. Trust me. Scholarships dry up after four years no matter how good your grades are. I can't afford another two years to be a doctor.*

If she'd ever thought about medical school, it was more of a fantasy, rather like winning the lottery or becoming the queen of England. She had equal chances of either happening. For a very brief time, she'd played with the idea of being doctor. Ogden had brought it up, though not intentionally. As far as she could tell, she'd be ten times a better doctor than he was. She'd certainly have a better bedside manner.

I agree. Clayton's voice sounded in her head again.

Nora tried to keep her face from showing her aggravation. Did she not have a single private thought?

Nora, my girl, when will you accept what is? We are soul mates destined to be together throughout time. We are not meant to be separate. Together we are stronger than apart. Surely, you've heard the old story how the Gods tore us apart in their jealousy.

She found her head nodding. Nana had told her the story with fervency, believing the Gods had played the same trick on her, separating her from Grandfather Buell. Luckily, they'd managed to find each other again.

The image of her grandparents dancing together, looking lovingly into each other's eyes, almost made her tear up. Good Goddess, she didn't need that. Any more dramatics and she might end up on the curb before her stop. It did happen. It was more like a suspension, though. The offenders were back within a week.

With two loving grandparents who have managed to transcend the boundaries of time, why do you not believe? Why can you not accept we are soul mates?

Nora could almost see his handsome face and lifted eyebrows. Why couldn't she accept he was communicating through time when so much had happened in her family's life that should make her believe? It wasn't that she didn't believe people could pass through centuries, something like walking through a cosmic revolving door. Oddly, *that* she could believe. It was the part about having a soul mate. She'd never expected one. Maybe she'd felt undeserving after the incident.

Those animals would go missing if I were in your time.

Nora bit her lip. She never knew when Clayton was eavesdropping on her. There were things she'd rather he didn't know.

Do not blame me for that. Your thoughts came to me, so strongly it was as if you were screaming. How could I not hear? Remember, you didn't do anything wrong. As much as I hate to leave you now, I've arrived in a town with sickness so I cannot converse any longer.

His voice and presence disappeared from her head, leaving a little empty-inside feeling. She'd keep that information to herself. Plenty of people would make jokes about losing her marbles if they knew.

Chapter Six

The diner came into sight. Thank the Goddess. Her arm was stiff after twenty minutes of swinging from the bus strap. The seats she'd hoped would open up hadn't.

The crowded diner parking lot indicated there would no downtime for her. She sprinted across the pavement, trying to work the stiffness out of her arm by making circles with it. No sooner did she open the door than Ernie called out.

"Glad you're here. Get suited up. I could use the help."

Great. Not exactly what she wanted to hear, but it kept her mind occupied. The smell of frying hamburger and bacon made her mouth water. Was she drooling like a dog at the thought of food? The thought distracted her as she walked in the direction of the restroom and right into the path of a customer who stood up, bumping into her. A brush of chilling evil touched her. Her flesh cringed as she pulled away. Weird, rather like one of those cartoons when a character goes bad and a dark smoke starts spreading through the cartoon body until it is all black. The urge to wash her bare arm where she'd been touched overwhelmed her.

On the bus, in the elevator, even at the university, she brushed against people all the time without this reaction. Her eyes traveled up to meet those of her least-favorite customer.

"So good to see you, Nora." Mr. Creepy lingered on her name as if caressing it. Yuk. He'd probably intentionally stood so she'd blunder into him.

Nora bobbed her head. Anxious to escape, she continued to the bathroom, dodging a toddler who darted out from a booth.

Before the incident, she hadn't recognized evil. She'd assumed most people were pretty much the same, no worse or better than anyone else. Sure, a few were mean-spirited, while others were more kind, but that was the extent. Maybe that's what she'd wanted to believe. When she'd found herself helpless against evil, she'd decided her best bet was to play it safe, especially when she sensed evil nearby. But that man packed maliciousness in a huge, invisible suitcase, he carried everywhere. Why was she the only one who saw it?

Rushing into the tiny bathroom, she locked the door. The owner didn't like the staff to spend too much time in the non-gender bathroom since it kept out patrons. By the time she'd stripped her top off and turned on the hot water, the hammering began.

"Give me a minute," she yelled in the direction of the closed door, hoping the person would take a hint. Pumping a big glob of the antiseptic soap into her hand, she lathered her torso and arms with it. Wiping down with the wet rough paper towels left brown paper crumbs behind. She felt no cleaner. Maybe she should wipe her legs down, too.

The hammering started up again, along with a voice. "Hey, I have to go. That chili went through me like water."

Not what the other customers in the diner would want to hear.

Nora shrugged on her chef smock, not taking time to close the top two buttons before grabbing her backpack and opening the door to a red-faced woman. "Sorry," she mumbled as she squeezed around the woman.

You'd think a restaurant would have two restrooms big enough to accommodate more than one person at a time. The thought preoccupied her until she swung open the kitchen door.

Ernie half-turned from his place at the grill. "It's about time—" He stopped talking, and his eyes dropped.

Nora looked down as well. Her smock gaped open, exposing her modest cleavage. Oh, my. Her fingers immediately buttoned the opening as her face reddened. Did he think she'd done that on purpose to catch his attention or something? Goddess, she hoped not. Not knowing what to do, she decided to go with pretending nothing had happened at all. "Wow, big crowd out there. Still conventioneers?"

Ernie turned to flip the almost-done hamburgers and lifted the crisp bacon onto a paper towel to blot the grease. He answered without facing her and grumbled the words. "Some, but our regulars are here, along with your favorite, who refused to order until you arrived. Didn't want to take a chance on me fixing his food."

Nora mentally added what he didn't say: *Screw you, you nasty, foul, evil creature.*

Okay, maybe Ernie wasn't thinking that. It was just her. Perhaps she'd burn his food today. Of course, he'd insist on talking to her about it. Might even complain to the manager. Barb would act as if she cared while he complained, but would laugh about it later. Herman, the owner, tended to react impulsively. He would fire Nora without a second thought. The same way he'd let Susan, a third-shift waitress, go when a customer had complained she was unfriendly. What he didn't say was Susan had slapped his hand when he tried to grope her. There was a good chance she would never know why she lost her position.

In Indiana, as well as several other states, employers could hire and fire at will. A person could hire whomever they wanted, no matter how unqualified they were. The owner could fire you if he didn't like your eye shadow as long as he didn't tell you. Legitimate complaints against firing could merit unemployment, which cost the company. It was best to give no reason for firing. No intelligent boss would admit he fired someone because she was old, smelly, ugly, or overweight, but many did. A few were dumb enough to admit it and ended up in the newspaper and in court for discrimination. She didn't know about Herman. He'd never struck her as smart or particularly interested in the diner. The diner ran well despite his interference, thanks to Barb.

It would be nice not be around Mr. Creepy. Thoughts of him caused her to open her paper cook hat too vigorously, tearing it. Ernie gave her another hat from the shelf over the grill without comment. As much as Mr. Creepy bothered her, there were bound to be men just like him elsewhere. Getting a job in a college town was no easy thing with the huge pool of available students to work. The diner always worked with her hours, which was more than most places would do. She'd just have to suck it up and deal with it.

Glancing at the order slips, she dropped some fries and chicken strips into the hot oil. Grabbing six plates, she placed them on the wooden prep bar to ready them for their eventual burgers and fries. People gladly paid a few bucks more for a simple fast-food meal served on a real plate with a dill spear on the side. Could be it wasn't the food that brought them, but the atmosphere. It was far from a trendy place, but there was a mellow aspect about the diner that no one was in a hurry. Lonely people could pretend the chatty server really was their friend, all for the price of a modest tip.

Nora supposed the diner was better than some restaurants. The fact they didn't serve alcohol eliminated most of the drunks. Staying open almost twenty-four hours brought in some interesting characters in the middle of the night, but by that time, she was asleep and dreaming.

The vividness of her dreams lately troubled her, as well as the possibility they might not entirely be dreams.

She put the open buns on the left side of the plate, allowing enough room to slide the fries in place. Placing the lettuce leaf carefully on top of the open bun top, she followed it with a tomato slice.

Why did the nocturnal meetings bother her? If she were honest with herself, she'd admit they were the most pleasant aspect of her life, wedging in between work, school, the hospital, and dodging Ogden. Clayton had been nothing but nice to her, she thought, as she placed a dill spear near the edge of a plate. An onion slice followed the tomato as the sandwich waited for the sizzling patty.

An alarm buzzed, alerting her that the fries needed attention. Flipping them into the metal container that allowed the oil to drip off, she wondered if Clayton was a figment of her imagination. She'd been having the dreams for years, but had always had trouble remembering the details. Often, she'd awake with a sense of security that seemed to be woefully missing from her life.

Why were the dreams becoming so vivid now? Was she astral traveling in her sleep? Could you astral travel to other times? Whom would she ask? Her grandfather was her best bet, but he'd ask questions. She'd not put it past him to probe her mind—for her own good, he'd explain.

Ernie called out, "Get a move on with those fries or the order will get cold."

Using the scoop, she measured huge helpings of fries onto each plate. Another reason people came to the diner. Fries cost the restaurant almost nothing. It was surprising most restaurants were so stingy with them.

Her schooling required she take a variety of psychology classes to help understand her future patients. She often used the information she obtained in class on customers and even co-workers. She shoved another serving of fries on the plate, mounding it high. The customers enjoyed seeing a full plate. It made them think they got reward or a favor. The same plate served by a smiling server made the customer feel special. It was probably better than some paper-wrapped mystery food that a fast-food employee pushed across the counter.

Taking off her food-service gloves, she stacked the plates on her arms. No way could she carry the plates with the slippery gloves on. She approached the window with the food and called out, "Order up, Robin."

It was important to acknowledge the right server to prevent someone from snatching up specials meant for someone else. There was some rivalry among the waitresses to serve their customers first. Nora couldn't understand the backstabbing attitude, but she'd never belonged to the mean-girls club. Using what she learned in class, she could diagnose the women as having a fear of scarcity with a touch of paranoia. They might believe there were not enough good tippers to go around, while fearing the possible loss of their job.

Returning to the grill, she donned fresh gloves. Looking at the newest orders, she laid out seven frozen patties on the grill. "How much longer are you staying, Ernie?"

"How's the crowd?" He used the edge of the spatula to sweep the grease into the catcher.

"All the booths are full, but no one is waiting. I'd say it is slowing down." That was good, because she didn't want Ernie staying over his shift. Barb might expect other cooks to help in a rush, but that didn't mean they received any compensation for it. It was a common-courtesy deal.

The cook slid one burger away from the rest and gestured to it. "Want to spit on this one? We'll make sure it goes to your admirer."

The suggestion shocked Nora. A nervous giggle escaped as she shook her head. "Um, no. I can see myself villainized on social media in a heartbeat. I'll give it a mental spit and be good."

Ernie laughed and pushed the burger back into the company of the rest of the patties. "Just ignore him. As long as you stay behind the counter, there's no way he can touch you. Besides, there's plenty of cops who stop here, too. If you ever feel unsafe, call someone to come get you."

Nora smiled at the cook's attempt to give her fatherly advice. "Thanks, Ernie."

She didn't bother to tell him there was no one she could call. Neither she nor Tonya owned a car. No way would she call Ogden. Of course, with Ogden, half the time he'd tell her it was a bad time and he couldn't make it. As boyfriends went, he sucked.

Perhaps that was why she'd created Clayton. He was everything she wanted in a man but never expected to get. Like her father, she could depend on him. He'd never let her down. He was funny, charming, and not too hard on the eyes. It was odd that she'd envisioned him in a different century.

I'll have you know you did not make me up.

Clayton's indignant tone almost caused her to drop the plate in her hand. Sliding the plate on the metal window ledge, she said, "Order up."

She made the mistake of glancing toward her least-favorite customer. He looked up at the same time and waved. Inhaling deeply, she backed away from the window. She so didn't need this.

Need what?

Nora's head swung toward Ernie, who was untying his apron. True, she didn't want to talk to Clayton in front of the cook, but carrying on a conversation in her head while she was alone wouldn't be much better.

Remember, you don't have to voice your thoughts, since I can hear them.

"Oh, joy," she grumbled more to herself than Clayton.

Ernie threw his greasy apron in the laundry, but looked up at her words. "Wha'd ya say?"

Nora scrambled for an appropriate reply. "Could you give Mr. Creepy a shove out the door on the way out?"

"Love to, but I always go out the back door." He suited his actions to his words and headed for the door. "See ya."

"Yeah." Nora held up her hand in reply. She turned to the stove, where bacon sizzled and a few burgers steamed as they defrosted. Any normal person working so long around meat would have become a vegetarian, but not her. It could be a sign of something being not quite right about her. That and hearing voices in her head.

Will you stop debasing yourself, darling? I already explained we are soul mates, which means we function as one.

Nora flipped the bacon while trying to direct her thoughts. *What if I don't want to be part of your soul-mate oneness?*

I am truly hurt. If you felt that way, you should have made your decision seven lifetimes ago.

They'd known each other for seven lifetimes. How long had she lived? Maybe the better question was: How many lifetimes had she had?

Not sure how many lifetimes you've had, but I've had nine. Let me tell you, two were so bitter and bleak without you by my side I was determined to find you in this life. No matter where you were. Life wasn't worth a handful of cold spit without you by my side.

Nora wrinkled her nose. *You almost had me tearing up until the spit remark.*

Well, it's true. Without you, my life consists of waiting for you to appear. When I tired of waiting, I tried searching across the centuries.

Scooping the burgers up with the spatula, she flipped them. She chased the diced onions one customer requested across the grill. That would explain her eyes watering. *Why don't I remember any of the lives we've spent together?*

A sudden silence from Clayton made her wonder if he had disappeared to attend to other duties, or maybe her imagination had run out of the ability to create dialogue for her imaginary friend. Then his warm voice returned, sounding a bit melancholy.

I wondered that myself. I wasn't born knowing you, but gradually there would be dreams of a dark-haired lass named Nora. Along with the dream came memories about who we had been in centuries past. At first, I told no one, thinking they were just dreams. Strange ones, but dreams. I met a conjuring woman who told my fortune for a few coins. She spoke of you by name and the love we shared of centuries past. She convinced me I could find you. I felt you recognized me the first time you traveled through time. Do you not know me, lass?

A hard question she didn't know how to answer. She corralled the onions to place them on the waiting burger then topped it with cheese. She had a few regulars who had special orders. Another reason they came here as opposed to buying fast food. No matter how many other restaurants sang about having it your way, the customer seldom did. That cut into the assembly-line process.

She carried the finished plate to the window and simply rang the bell, since only one waitress was still on duty. Lorraine had stayed only until the shift fully changed over and the drawer counted.

Once she stepped back into the kitchen, she flipped her two remaining burgers and dumped the remaining fries into the drainer.

How did she feel about Clayton?

I felt safe with you when I hadn't felt safe in a long time. It felt like I belonged in your arms, and you would never hurt me.

Nora caught herself hugging her arms around herself as if surrounded by Clayton's embrace. The bread man could show up while she was embracing herself. She immediately dropped her arms.

You felt safe in my arms because I would protect you with my very life, and I have in the past.

A pang squeezed her heart, and her hand rested lightly on her chest. She knew without asking that Clayton had died more than once to protect her.

I believe you worked so hard at forgetting or at least burying the bad things in this life that you also stymied the memories of us from coming through. Only when you were asleep and your mind was at rest could I reach you before.

Nora plated up the last three orders and carried them to the window. Just her luck, she had the ideal boyfriend in the wrong century.

Would you be uncomfortable with a Wiccan girlfriend?

She'd never confessed to Ogden any of her beliefs. She knew how he'd react. He'd tell her it was something she needed to get rid of, rather like a pair of old shoes.

I am not sure what Wiccan means. If you are okay with me having a touch of the fey about me, then I am sure I am fine with a Wiccan, although I wouldn't be wanting a girlfriend.

What did he mean by not wanting a girlfriend? He was the one who'd called them soul mates. She was about to ask when the bread man swung open the back door. While he wasn't as chatty as the milk guy was, he did merit some attention. By the time she had signed the invoice, she realized Clayton had disappeared without another word. How strange.

CHAPTER SEVEN

The bread man slammed the door as he left. She wasn't sure why, but suddenly the idea that anyone could walk into the kitchen began to bug her. Tall metal shelving units with boxes of Styrofoam ware and napkins filled the wall behind her along with the walk-in fridge. There really wasn't any place to hide, unless someone was willing to stay in the fridge. The culprit would have had to slip in and conceal himself while no one was in the kitchen. The kitchen wasn't empty often, especially since cooks usually stayed around an additional twenty or thirty minutes, helping or shooting the breeze. Nora was probably one of the few who left almost immediately, due to the bus schedule.

The stainless steel counters and wooden prep station didn't have any excess spaces a person could duck behind. The tall rack of buns pushed into the farthest corner of the room offered some possibility. Nora pulled the bread rack away from the wall and closer to the lights. Sure, it was awkward in the middle of the room, but she'd push it back before she left. Part of her mind thought she was being paranoid and ridiculed her for it, but another part wasn't so sure.

Taking a wet towel, she wiped down her workstation while she waited for an order. Accustomed to working alone, she used the time to recite medical information, keeping her voice low enough not to be heard in the diner. No one needed to hear her rattle off the names of bones or various muscle groups. Might cause them to wonder what she was cooking. Was it hamburger or something else? Other times she used the empty hours to contemplate her future home with a little garden and potted flowers lining the walk. The house didn't matter as much as wanting the stability a house represented.

Bonnie laughter carried to the kitchen. The second-shift waitress enjoyed her job, if her laughter was any indication. Her teased hair, heavily made-up eyes, and smock zipper pulled low enough to reveal her bountiful cleavage made her a stereotype. Still, Bonnie had regulars who enjoyed her calling them "hon" and "darling." Nora wasn't sure how old she was, but oddly enough, she felt the woman might be closer to her own age than she'd originally suspected. The hair and the liberal application of makeup aged the woman. It was almost as if she were disguising herself for work every night. The idea intrigued Nora, causing her to step through the swinging door that separated the kitchen from the diner, and watch Bonnie work. She might as well, since there were no orders coming her way.

A middle-aged couple had just finished their meal and were pushing themselves up out of the low booth. The man helped the woman up with a smile. Perhaps they were on a date. Not the classiest place in the world, but it served its purpose, especially if the guy wasn't that invested in his date. They walked to the cash register, conversing in low voices. The man turned toward the woman, listening to her while she spoke as if he cared about what she said. Curious to check out the couple more closely, she called out, "I'll get the cash register."

Using the gate that separated the service area from the booths, she passed Bonnie to reach the register.

The woman looked up from her conversation with a cop to give her a grateful smile. "Thanks, hon."

Nora squeezed past her in the narrow service alley, thinking if any of the servers gained weight, there'd be no way they could pass each other. Her glance flickered over the cop and Bonnie. The server leaned over the counter to pour the tired-looking man more coffee. His uniform stated he was a cop, but his posture, along with the frown lines in his face, announced he didn't enjoy being one. Ironically, the same uniform he probably disliked wearing had Bonnie fluttering over him like a bee on a sunflower. Bonnie was a big fan of uniforms, though not because of the authority, they represented, but rather it was an indication of a stable job.

Nora took the bill from the man and rang it up. The wide gold band on his finger caught her eye, confirming the two were married. The woman placed her hand on her husband's arm possessively and moved closer.

Swallowing the urge to inform the woman that she had no interest in her husband, Nora handed the change back. "Have a nice evening, you two."

The man's eyes twinkled. "How can it be anything but good when I'm married to the best woman in the world?"

His wife simpered and looked up at him adoringly.

Nora's breath caught in her throat. How sweet. Sometimes she forgot married people could be like that. Most of the married ones who came in either ate in a sullen silence, bickered throughout the meal, or tried to balance caring for all their young children while trying to feed themselves. Many of the younger couples spent more time looking at their cell phone screens than each other.

The bell rang as four men came into the diner, their paint-dotted white uniforms revealing their profession. Four orders coming up, she thought as she made her way to the kitchen. The bell rang again, announcing more customers. Her hand was spread flat on the kitchen door, ready to push it open, when she hesitated. An image of an unknown man lying in wait with a chef's knife in hand ready to plunge it into her back flooded her mind.

Her body felt frozen. Turning her head toward Bonnie took real effort. "I am going in the kitchen to make the orders you'll be giving me soon."

The server handed the four men menus, but glanced up to give Nora a baffled stare. "Okay, you'll be getting those orders real soon, too."

Nothing for it, she'd have to go into the kitchen. No one had any use for a short-order cook who was afraid of the kitchen. It sounded like a joke, but unfortunately, she had no punch line. Pushing the door open, she found the same fluorescent-lighted kitchen as before with the strong odor of onions and grease. The sound of a door closing caused her heart to skip a beat. Her eyes flew to the back door that remained firmly shut. She took five fast steps to the door and locked it. The deliveries were over for the night, which meant there was no reason for it to be unlocked.

Taking the spatula, she scraped the old grease from the grill, prepping it for the next orders. The sound of a door closing again caught her attention. Nora realized with a sigh that it was the restroom door, which was directly across from the kitchen. Countless times over innumerable shifts, she'd heard the door open and close, but now she was as nervous as a long-tailed cat caught at a rocking-chair marathon. Paranoid, that's what she was.

Bonnie banged the bell, indicating orders. The thin slips of paper waved from their clips. Snatching them, Nora wondered why Bonnie couldn't call out the orders. The bell irritated her, making her feel like some trained animal. Go get the orders, prepare the food, put it in the window, and make sure to ring the stupid bell. Her level of irritability surprised her.

Placing three frozen patties on the grill, she tried to analyze her own behavior. Things had been hectic with her college career ending. Soon, she'd be out doing the things she'd spent so much time planning to do. Most people would have been excited and frightened at the same time. Those not quite ready to meet the real world packed the graduate programs. Despite the university's assurances that additional education was always beneficial, graduate students educated themselves out of getting a startup position. The lower the degree the less they were paid, which explained hospitals' preferences for hiring those with the basic ones. In a bizarre way, they made their fears of not finding a job a reality by over-educating themselves.

Squatting, she removed the bacon, eggs, and cheese from the under-the-counter fridge. Placing the six strips of bacon beside the burgers to sizzle, she returned to her contemplation. Sure, she was uncertain, but she wanted to get on with her life. She'd been in a holding pattern too long. Her unease was probably more about Ogden than anything. Emotionally, she'd withdrawn from him but had failed to tell him they were finished. He'd find someone else to be his servant girl. The thought eased her guilt but simultaneously turned her stomach.

For the last two days, she'd cold-shouldered him. Had he called her? Sent her flowers? Show up at her apartment or work begging to know what was wrong? No, of course not. That would have required some work on his part.

Grabbing the seasoning container, she liberally shook the can. Working the spatula under the burgers, she flipped them with vigor, splashing grease on herself. No good getting worked up over Ogden. Count it as a lesson learned.

"Stupid horse's ass," she growled.

Why couldn't she have someone who loved her for who she was as opposed to what she could do for him? Her eyes narrowed at the burgers as if they were the cause of her problems. After testing the burgers with her spatula, she started the eggs. The men would expect their orders at the same time, even though the burgers took longer to cook. Timing was the hardest part of her job, especially when working alone. She held the egg up, ready to crack it open on the metal counter, when Clayton's voice sounded in her head.

I love you. I have for centuries. It doesn't matter what body you take, because your soul is the same, and that's what I love.

The egg slipped from her fingers to spatter on the floor. "Shit." She didn't have time to clean it up and get the food ready. Grabbing the salt container, she shook it over the oozing mess for easier cleaning later, a trick she'd learned from Nana. The salt absorbed the liquid and made it sweepable, as opposed to requiring mopping. Once she got the food plated, she'd deal with it. Bending to get another egg, she mentally asked, *Are you going to say something else outrageous that will cause me to drop the egg?*

Not getting an answer, she proceeded to crack the eggs into a greased skillet. Ernie always cooked the eggs on the grill, leaving them with a slight beefy tone. He called the griddle the great equalizer because all protein mingled on it. He jokingly referred to Nora as a segregationist since she used a skillet for the eggs.

Clayton's continued silence bothered her, unsure if he was miffed or just not talking. The fry buzzer rang as soon as she had the burgers plated. The toast popped up by the time the fries were on the plate. Damn, she was good. Well, at least when it came to timing food.

Placing the plates in the window, she hit the bell twice, drawing an irritated gaze from Bonnie. Slipping back into the kitchen, she knelt to clean up the egg. When she swept the salt-saturated mess into the dustpan, Clayton spoke.

I could use your help here. There's an epidemic, and I could use another pair of hands.

This wasn't a conversation they'd had before, which puzzled her, but she could hear the strain in his voice.

Nora, I am sorry. That makes me sound no better than all those other people who used you. I do love you more than life itself. I've proved it over several lifetimes. Right now, this illness has me whipped. I don't know what to do.

He'd loved her over several lifetimes. What she wouldn't give to remember their lives together.

How can I help you? She asked him.

The anguish that had flavored his words, and the weary tone of his voice, indicated low energy. An image of Clayton formed with his shoulders drooping and his jaunty smile replaced by a grim, determined visage. His rolled-up sleeves and missing vest indicated a long day, probably one without a break or assistance. Clayton still managed a soft litany of encouraging words as he labored over a sick child whose fever-ravaged body tossed in delirium.

Did she really see Clayton somehow or did she imagine the scene?

His voice remained silent as she refilled the cook fridge for the next shift. Slamming the fridge door in frustration, she looked around for tasks to busy herself until her shift was complete. Buns, yeah, she'd grab a couple of bags to place above the grill. That done, she placed her hands on her hips and stared at the mute stainless steel appliances and wire racks piled high with Styrofoam takeout boxes. Oddly enough, they didn't have too many takeout orders. People came to the diner because they wanted to sit. Besides, the diner didn't have a drive-through. By the time someone came in, placed an order, and waited for it, a person could have enjoyed a beverage and spent the time with a companion chatting. It explained the unopened tower of takeout trays in their plastic sleeves.

Nora tidied the boxes on the rack, thinking the cleaning was a waste of her time. Clayton needed her and the medical knowledge she had in her head. Her hands fisted as she considered how many elderly or young were dying even now in Clayton's century. The young and the elderly were often the first victims in an epidemic. The young often hadn't built up the immunity to fight off the diseases, while the elderly didn't have the strength to resist. Why was she here when she needed to be there?

Throwing her hands in the air, she spoke to the empty kitchen. "What use is it to study medicine when I can't use what I know?"

Bonnie's unnaturally bright red hair flashed into view as the server stuck her head in the pass-through window. "Something wrong back there?"

Great. Just what she needed, her co-worker doubting her stability. "Nope," Nora called and used her foot to jiggle the rack holding the trays until one stack slipped off, hitting the floor with a hollow-sounding plop. "It's these boxes. Not stacked right. One fell off and hit me in the face."

"Oh, is that all?" Bonnie's voice registered her disinterest as her head disappeared from the window.

Nora was good with Bonnie's lack of concern. The server probably experienced enough in the school of hard knocks that she didn't have any interest in worrying about other people. That was okay with Nora. Worried people poked into her business. Sure, everyone would be cool with the voices-in-her-head story. If the state hadn't closed its state-run mental hospital, she'd end up in a padded cell faster than she could say, "Bob's my uncle." Nope, it was best to keep the strange and bizarre info close.

Pushing the rack into place, she bent to pick up the stack she'd knocked free.

Now, if someone thought a person was loony tuney, they either had to criminalize their behavior so the penal system would lock them away or have wads of money to put them in a private facility. Since she fell into neither category, she was on her own, rather like the woman who sang arias while grocery shopping. The well-groomed woman had a nice voice, and she was no more disturbing than people muttering into their cell phones and definitely better than the tired mothers threatening to rip off their children's arms and beating them with it.

Her voices…make that, Clayton's voice was mild compared to most people's idiosyncrasies. Her feet carried her to the pass-through window to check to see if their favorite alien abductee was in the house. He was. He kept a transistor radio plugged into his ear tuned to some news station that confused anyone trying to scan his mind. He cautioned the diner employees to do the same. Yep, she was the sane one here, but just in case, she'd call Grandpa Buell.

If anyone understood how to time travel, he did. Maybe he could explain her growing apprehension about the door, too. She'd have to explain about Clayton's voice in her head, which would almost feel like she was divulging a secret, hers and Clayton's. Still, she could depend on Grandpa to tell no one. He understood without words, which made it helpful. How much he knew might be an issue, too. Would he know she found herself growing fonder and fonder of this man trapped in the past or that she found Clayton's eyes and hair super sexy? That wouldn't do.

The door chimed, indicating someone had entered. Good, it would keep her busy. A quick peek showed it was Brandon. The wall clock revealed he was a good forty minutes early.

Seeing her, he waved. "Hey, Cookie," he said with a wide grin. "Think you can whip me up a three-egg omelet with cheese?"

His nickname for her came from his days in the service when they referred to the cook as Cookie. It seemed odd that a Marine would welcome Cookie as a nickname, but they'd also called the gunnery sergeant Gunnie. Maybe rough soldiers needed something playful in their lives.

Brandon sat at the counter with his muscular arms crossed and resting on the top. The man stayed in shape. As if noticing her perusal, he winked.

Flustered, Nora ducked out of the window view, but still answered, "Omelet coming up."

Cracking the eggs into the blender, she wondered about Brandon's behavior. Had he always been that flirtatious? Couldn't be. She'd have given him the cold shoulder the way she did all men who tried to flirt with her. What was different about him?

Maybe he'd ended a relationship and was on the rebound. The reticent cook never talked much about his personal life. The Marine tattoo on his biceps initially announced his military connection. Then again, it could be her. What if she was changing? Was it possible?

The sound of the blender whipping the egg mixture into a frothy mass filled the tiny kitchen. Ladling a tablespoon of oil into the skillet, she shook it to coat the pan. Turning off the blender, she removed it from the stainless steel base and poured the eggs into the waiting skillet. A few shakes of the spice canister added the right amount of salt, pepper, and a few other spices she couldn't identify. It was part of the diner's secret, along with the blender. Sliding the skillet rapidly across the grill, she kept the eggs from sticking to the sides.

When had she signaled that she might be open to flirtation? Tonya had teased her that she'd give an iceberg a run for its money when it came to being frosty. The comment had pleased her, since it was the effect she wanted. It was hard to remember what she'd been like before the incident, since so much effort went into forgetting that time.

She'd never been the perky cheerleader type, but she did remember being friendly and helpful. The Wiccan Rede was: Do as you please but harm none. Nana translated it to mean to help others if possible. Nora did help others in the not so distant past. It left her with a happy, satisfied feeling. At the time, she'd felt safe in announcing her beliefs. Not in the in-your-face way some teens did, constantly questioning your eternal destination. A tiny pentacle had graced her neck, but it might as well have read "Satan's Whore", considering the impression some of the boys had received.

Grabbing the skillet handle, she lifted the pan and gave it a good shake before placing the cheese on the omelet.

She'd done nothing wrong then. The nurse had told her the same thing almost six years ago, but she hadn't believed it. Instead, after reading countless accounts of sexual assaults, she'd realized none of the women had invited it. People would point fingers at victims, claiming they shouldn't have been at the party, the grocery, the park, or wherever the attack happened.

Nora had tried to analyze her own behavior, trying to discover the inciting factor. As a result, she'd sheared off her long hair that one of her attackers used to hold her down. Her clothes had become as conservative as any primitive religious sect's, with high necklines and dark colors. The only difference was she wore pants. Overall, she made no effort to be attractive. She froze out men who tried to get past her initial barriers.

There were always one or two who tried, convinced she was a challenge. A few others labeled her a dyke and felt a conversion was in order. Dissuading the last type had been the whole reason behind Ogden, but he'd never served his purpose. He was just another man who used her. Goddess knew she'd had enough of that.

The toast popped up as she slid the omelet on the plate. She arranged the toast on the plate with a few slices of tomato, which she knew Brandon liked.

She'd settled for Ogden only because she'd never expected to have a real-live relationship. The love songs that portrayed a man who was so hopelessly smitten he'd do anything for the woman he loved? Nope, she'd never expected that.

Grabbing the plate, she backed into the hall door to deliver the plate herself. No other customers were there, which would allow her a few minutes to talk.

The same behavior in someone else she might have regarded as flirting, but she considered it more of an experiment. She centered the plate in front of Brandon with a smile. A ridiculous urge to whip off her paper hat and ruffle her fingers through her hair came over her. She quelled it, knowing she had a good thirty minutes left on her shift. Was this how normal women felt when around an available man?

It probably was. The part she'd frozen thawed a little. Clayton had told her she needed healing. Turned out, he was right. It was healing as well as forgiving— herself. Living the way she had for the past years no longer seemed appealing. Closed off to everyone, including her family, to keep her hurt private was not the way she wanted to live. It'd happened. She'd survived, and now she wanted the life she'd been so busy denying herself.

Why couldn't she have a man who loved her? Her lips tipped up at the thought of sleeping in loving arms.

A nudge against her arm caught her attention. Brandon's eyes stared into hers, making her wonder if she'd done or mentioned something that had given away her most recent thoughts. Sliding off the stool, she shrugged her shoulders and teased. "I better go get the kitchen cleaned. The next cook is a real hard-ass."

Brandon's laughter rang out behind her. It was good she could make him laugh, but she didn't want to encourage him too much. It was never good for co-workers to date. Barb discouraged the waitresses from dating the customers, too. A rejected customer would abstain from visiting the diner, but could also bad-mouth the place out of spite.

Another six months and she'd be out of here, and no one would request she make a cheeseburger with extra onions, again. All she needed to do was stay friends with Brandon.

Grabbing the rag soaked in bleach water, she rubbed it over all the surfaces, disinfecting them. Good thing the cooks wore white or their uniforms would have been dotted with faded spots. The smell made her crinkle her nose a little, and she wondered how Clayton disinfected in his time. Did they disinfect?

The door creaked open, catching her attention. She spun on her heel with the rag clutched to her chest. The fight-or-flight response had taken hold. Always a big proponent of flight, she still considered the weapons at hand: a skillet and a chef's knife, both formidable.

Brandon walked through the door with an easy gait. Her racing pulse slowed. She glanced up at the clock, aware her shift hadn't ended yet. Her upheld hand with the threatening cloth in it dropped to her side. Nothing too threatening here, which made her feel a tad ridiculous, but being on her guard had kept her safe all through college. She tossed the rag back in the improvised pickle tub bucket.

"Your shift doesn't start for another twenty minutes." She turned her back on him to go back to scraping the grill. While most of the patrons had nothing against grease, they preferred their artery-clogging fat to be fresh.

Brandon came up close behind her, causing the desire to flee to return.

"Go on out. I came back to fix you something before you leave. This way, you won't miss your bus." Brandon's arm reached past her head to grab a paper hat.

Nora ducked under his arm to put some distance between them. Obviously, she hadn't gotten over her aversion to men in her personal space. Why should he be in her space? She stared at his back, outlined by his tight white T-shirt. Brandon chose not to wear a chef smock. Ernie joked that if he worked out as much as Brandon did, he'd want to show it off, too, by wearing a tight T-shirt rather than a chef smock.

"Barb might come in and check," Nora said.

His head twisted enough for her to see the arch of one raised, disbelieving eyebrow. "I know she never comes out once she gets home anymore."

Technically, Barb was supposed to check in twice a night. In the beginning, she had, but once all the troublesome elements left or were helped out, she no longer bothered. Occasionally, she'd come back on the weekends with her husband and to eat free.

Brandon continued to hold her gaze. "How about it?"

She was about to defer when she thought, Why not? It was hard to remember someone doing something nice for her without any expectations.

"Okay." She crumpled her paper hat and flung it into the trash. Whipping the apron over her head, she aimed it at the laundry bag.

As she opened the side door, Brandon caught it with his hand, holding it open, causing his bicep to bunch. His tattoo was at her eye level, filling her immediate view with the word "Marines." Blinking, she managed to tear her eyes away from the tattoo and up to his face.

His eyes laughed a little before he asked, "What do you want?"

Nora hesitated, biting her bottom lip. It felt like he was asking her more than if she wanted a burger or chicken fingers. It was probably her imagination. "Surprise me."

Except for two lone men at separate booths, both nursing cups of coffee with their plates pushed aside, the diner was empty as she took a seat at the counter. She recognized them, not by name, but as the type of men who stretched their time out at the diner because they had nothing at home. Bonnie would talk to them, making them feel important and wanted, even if only for the tip they'd leave.

Bonnie approached her with a smirk and her favorite diet cola. When she reached the counter, she slid the drink toward her and looked back in the direction of the kitchen. She flattened her hand on the bar to balance herself as she half-leaned across the counter, better to whisper into Nora's ear, "What's going on with you and our favorite Marine?"

"Nothing." She took a few pulls on her straw. Why would Bonnie assume something was up? She hadn't done anything to encourage the man. At least, she didn't think she had.

The man in question appeared in the window. "Order up for my favorite short-order cook."

Bonnie threw her a knowing look before she picked up the plate. "Oh, what's this? I've never seen it on the menu."

Brandon had his forearms braced against the window as he watched the reactions to his creation. "I consider it a gourmet grilled cheese. I used two different cheeses, plus bacon and sliced tomatoes."

Bonnie made a smacking sound with her lips as she put the plate in front of Nora. "Nothing?" The waitress mouthed the word in a mocking fashion, well aware Brandon couldn't see or hear her.

What could Nora say? She hadn't done anything outside of her little experiment minutes earlier. "Thanks, Brandon. This looks good."

Bonnie walked away muttering, "Yum." Nora wasn't sure if she was talking about the sandwich or Brandon.

Taking a bite under the still-watching man's eyes, she chewed enthusiastically. "Hmm, that's good. It should be on the menu."

"No, it shouldn't." Brandon shook his head. "If it was on the menu, it wouldn't be special."

Oh, my. Nora wondered if her eyes got big. Talk about declaring his intent. She took another bite and continued to chew. When in doubt, eat. The sandwich was good, with the butter-crisped bread and the gooey cheese. The bacon added a salty bite, while the tomato complemented with a mild, juicy afternote. It was a delicious sandwich. Why this curious behavior now?

Clayton's voice returned. Hearing his familiar timber brought some reassurance considering his abrupt departure earlier. *I'm not liking this a bit. I am the one who is healing you, loving you, bringing you back to life. No need for that man jack to cast his eyes on you.*

The jealousy-flavored words sounded as if they were bitten out through clenched teeth. He thought he'd healed her. She wanted to object and explain she'd done any healing on her own, but she didn't. After the dreams she'd been having for years, though she seldom remembered them, she often awoke with a contented feeling. It could have been Clayton. Precious few other things could have caused her to wake with a smile.

That is right, darling. Remember that. You have loved me for lifetimes. Sure, and it has been difficult getting you to realize this almost every lifetime. I should be hurt that you've forgotten me so easily.

She didn't want to talk to Clayton under the watchful eyes of Bonnie, who kept smirking at her as she poured coffee for the lonely ones. It was odd that she'd forgotten, but Clayton had managed to get closer to her than anyone ever had. Would she have allowed that if she didn't recognize him?

No reason to work on convincing me, sweetheart. My jealousy of you working so close to a fine, strapping man overcame me.

How did he know about Brandon? Oh, yeah, it was all those walks he took around in her psyche. If she thought Brandon looked buff, then Clayton knew it.

This word "buff" makes no sense to me. All I know is you think about this Brandon more than I would like. I suspect he has his eye on you, too. Hard for me to imagine a man not being in love with you.

Nora fought rolling her eyes at his last remark, well aware no one knew she was conversing in her head. It wouldn't have looked any less odd if she'd chosen to explain it. Placing a tip by her plate, she made ready to leave. The growl of the diesel bus caused her to vault from her seat to catch her ride.

Running with her backpack dangling from her arm, she thanked the bus driver for his patience as she stepped in. It didn't matter that she'd been riding the same route for the last couple of years and left the diner at the same time. It never hurt to show gratitude.

CHAPTER EIGHT

The bus ride home was uneventful, if you considered having a voice in her head telling her how much he adored her as ordinary. Finally, Nora heaved a sigh and thought emphatically, *"Enough."*

It must have sounded like yelling. Her eternal soul mate went silent and left. The resulting sensation was similar to stepping on a butterfly, leaving her with a feeling of guilt.

She half-watched the woman across from her count her money. Nora considered telling her a bus wasn't a good place to flash a wad of bills. The dollars were oversized and almost neon green bright. Play money. The woman had play money, but treated it as if it were genuine. Some people might label her crazy, but money has only the value we give to it.

Love was like that, too. A woman in a nurse's smock rested her head against the seat with her eyes closed. The woman loved someone in her life. Could be a single parent trying to make a decent living to support a beloved child. The woman clutching her fake money was important to someone. At least, Nora hoped she was.

It wasn't as if Nora didn't have anyone. She had her family. She never doubted their love, but she still hoped for something more. Back before, she had been as frivolous as any teen, hoping to don a fancy dress to go to the prom with her favorite crush. On prom night, she'd taken a bag of chocolate-chip cookies and a book to visit Abby. She'd read to her friend of battling wizards, while her friend had wordlessly rocked back and forth.

Abby's parents had commended her for her devotion to her friend, which made her feel like a fraud. At the time, she'd felt somehow she was the reason Abby was behind thick walls adorned with trailing ivy. Now, she could place blame were it belonged. Maybe they'd both been too innocent and trusting. Nothing bad truly had touched their lives before then. How could they have recognized evil when it wore familiar faces?

Evil in its many forms was to blame. Misogynistic males considered every woman was theirs for the taking. The police who were supposed to help often doubted victims, as if they were part of some huge conspiracy to make men look bad. Even other women were quick to accuse the female victims of enticing the man somehow. It made as much sense as pedophiles accusing their seven-year-old victims of leading them on.

The knowledge that she hadn't caused the rape to happen lifted a weight off her shoulders, allowing her to sit a little straighter. Next time she visited her parents, she'd make a side trip to tell Abby they'd done nothing wrong. It might help. Evil lived in the world, and sometimes it settled in people. That had been her first hard, face-to-face encounter with it. She doubted it would be her last.

For years she'd battled with guilt and remembering, even hating the concept of physical love, connecting it all together. Rubbing her hands over her arms briskly, she chased away the goose bumps that formed whenever a memory of the night surfaced. It was her body's form of an early-warning system. Clayton was the key. Even though she hid her pain and shame from everyone else, it was more difficult when a person meandered through her mind, examining various thoughts. Apparently, what he found did not stop his devotion.

Closing her eyes, she recalled the feel of his arms around her as she'd cried. Never before had she permitted herself. Instead, she'd been angry and wary certain that the male gender could not be trusted. Crying in Clayton's embrace had released the pain. His reassurance that she was not to blame had allowed her to consider the idea.

Logically, she accepted that victims of sexual assault were not to blame, even if they went to the party, drank too much, or trusted the male who offered a ride home. She was willing to accept that other women didn't provoke their assault, but denied herself the same acceptance. What chance had she had to fight off the guys who had planned their attack? None. A couple of weeks ago, someone had sent her a newspaper article about one of her attackers being charged with the date rape of a woman he'd met speed dating. She suspected her nana had been the anonymous sender, but she didn't know for sure.

The bus slowed, indicating her stop was next. Once on the street, she looked around, practicing her usual caution in watching for anyone half-hidden in the shadows. She stuck two fingers through her meager key ring, brandishing the ragged edge of her apartment key as a weapon to use to claw out the eyes of potential attackers.

True, she had allowed the self-blame to slip away, but she'd still exercise her hard-earned caution to avoid being a repeat victim.

Staying inside the circles of lights the streetlights threw, she walked to her apartment. Tonya, probably hearing her on the stairs, threw the door open wide. "Well, hello, Mistress Carpenter."

From the way she sounded, coconut-flavored rum might have been on the menu tonight. "Good evening, Tonya. Everything okay?"

"Yesssssssh, why do you ask?" Her roommate clutched the door to hold herself upright. "You had a visitor while you were gone. Only a few hours after you left."

Nora squeezed in past her roommate. "Tonya, could you move? I don't want to catch your fingers in the door. Who was my visitor? Captain Morgan?" she asked, referring to the popular brand of rum.

"Ha, ha, aren't you the clever one?" Tonya took a few uncertain steps before plopping down on the couch and patting the seat beside her. "Come sit beside me and tell me what has put the smile on your face."

Nora perched on the edge of the couch, facing her buzzed roommate. "Who came by?"

"Ogden." She practically spat the word and then fell back into the couch cushions. "Lord have mercy. I knew he was a pompous jackass who considered himself better than God, but never had I ever spent so much time with the fool."

"What happened?" Ogden could be dry, snobby, and irritating, but she'd put up with it, feeling he served a purpose.

Tonya shook her head but moaned when the motion appeared to be too much for reeling senses. Instead, she propped her elbows on her knees to cradle her much-abused head. "You owe me big-time." Her hands and the position of her head muted the words.

An image of an angry Ogden raising his hand to her feisty roommate came to mind, immediately replaced by her roommate kneeing him, then threatening to do him more bodily harm with a dull knife. The man wouldn't have stood a chance. "He didn't hurt you, did he?"

Tonya's head lifted enough to pin Nora with a basilisk stare. "If you call being bored by his endless talk, then I was wounded savagely. How do you tolerate him?"

That was a good question. "Half the time I didn't even listen to him. Recently, I have been avoiding him altogether."

"Ah, yeah, that." Tonya rubbed a hand over her face as she struggled into a sitting position. "That's the problem. He decided to go out of his way and take time out of his busy schedule to check on you. He must have mentioned that at least ten times." She threw up her fingers several times, going past ten.

Nora decided not to mention her faulty counting skills in her present state. "So what did you say to him? How did you get him to leave?"

"It wasn't easy, let me tell you. After he finally heaved-ho, I decided to reward myself with a drink or two."

"Or three or four." Nora couldn't help from commenting.

Tonya groaned slightly before falling back on the couch. "You know the man. He will drive any person to drink. Surprised you're not an alcoholic from keeping company with him."

"We didn't keep that much company. It was more like he'd give me my orders for the day, and I'd do them." It sounded bad when she said it. She'd run errands for him for the privilege of being associated with the man. Ironically, no one had thought of the two of them as a pair, making the whole effort pointless.

"Yeah, well, that's what I tried to explain, that you were tired of the honor of playing Girl Friday for him."

Maybe Tonya had penetrated his thick hide of blue-blooded pride, whereas Nora could never nick it, not that she'd tried that much. "Did you convince him?"

"Not at first. It made no sense to him why you wouldn't want to continue doing his crap jobs." Tonya looked perplexed herself. She opened and closed her jaw a few times, popping it in the process.

"You'd think if he was so concerned, he'd shown up at the diner. Not that I want him to."

"Oh, yeah, that." Tonya scooched back into the cushion, trying to find a comfortable spot. She closed her eyes. Her mouth dropped open, and a snore emerged.

"Tonya, no sleeping until you tell me what you said." Nora pulled on her roommate's arm to get her attention.

The woman tried to shake her off before answering. "I told him you were letting the big buff Marine at the diner bang you. He went all red in the face. Said he'd see about that and stormed off." Tonya rolled onto her back and began snoring.

Nora couldn't believe her roomie could be so crude, but hey, Ogden could stretch anyone's patience. What had he meant when he'd said he'd see about that? Brandon's over-friendly manner suddenly made sense if Ogden had approached him and demanded to know if they were intimate.

Hard to know what Brandon's answer would have been. It should have been "absolutely not." If he'd been informed inadvertently, that someone, possibly her, had hitched their names together, would he have taken it, as she desired him?

Could her life get any more complicated?

"Really?" she demanded, but no one was awake to appreciate her ire.

Shaking out the afghan, she covered Tonya and slipped off her shoes.

Knowing Brandon as a man of few words, she figured he'd probably give a classic tough guy answer like, "None of your damn business," paired with a sly grin. Luckily, she had two days off before she had to return to the diner and deal with what Brandon might be thinking. It could have been he'd just been friendly tonight, but somehow she doubted it.

Assured her roommate was sleeping soundly, she decided it was time to call Grandpa. Closing her bedroom door, she dialed the number. Maybe it was silly hiding herself away in her room to talk, but it was a private conversation, one she didn't want to share even with her closest friend. Only Grandpa would understand, and possibly her younger sister, Leah. They were, after all, the only two time travelers she knew.

The phone rang four times, worrying Nora that her grandparents were already asleep. Maybe she should hang up before she woke them. The same time her finger hovered over the end button, her grandfather's voice sounded in her ear.

"Nora, sweetie, I've been waiting for your call."

His familiar voice relaxed her, bringing with it a sense of security and love. "How did you know?" Of course, he'd known she'd call the moment she'd thought about it. She probably had the only grandfather who could hear people's thoughts. Oh, he swore he didn't listen in, but he seemed to be tuned to the mention or thought of his name.

Nora looked at the phone curiously. Why did she bother with the device? But, then, she didn't have Grandpa Buell's ability.

"You had something to tell me about your young man."

Nora wondered whether he meant Ogden, although she'd never mentioned him, or Brandon, who was not her man, even though he may now think of himself as such. She hadn't said anything about him, either. The only thing she'd ever talked to Grandpa about was the dreams, which started as vague feelings of comfort and happiness. Sometimes the memory of a pair of kind eyes and a warm laugh were all that remained when she woke.

"Do you remember me talking to you about the dreams? As if someone, a guy, spoke to me as I slept?"

"Yes, I remember, child. That's who I was referring to when I called him your young man."

She could imagine her grandfather sitting with one leg crossed over the other, his white hair ruffled like Einstein's because he absent-mindedly ran his hands through it while thinking. It irritated Nana. She would try to smooth it down. He'd brush her hand way, declaring that people had to take him as they found him.

"Well, um, the dreams are coming more often. Every night. There are times when it seems so real I am convinced I am there. The other night I sat with him, talking by a campfire. The next morning, my clothes smelled like wood smoke."

"Hmm, did he say anything unusual to you?"

"He told me he was my soul mate and that we had been soul mates in several lifetimes. He told me he couldn't find me in his lifetime. He searched for me using divination methods and found me in another century." Instead of being freaked out by what she was saying, it all made sense somehow.

"Tell me about this young man who has an interest in you. I need to check him out. The better question is, how do you feel about all this?" Curiosity and sternness mingled in his voice. As the patriarch, he wanted to vet the man who would invade his granddaughter's dreams.

Biting her bottom lip, she considered her words. No need to dance around the topic, since Grandpa probably knew anyhow. "His name is Clayton McFane, and he's a healer."

"Irish name. Good chance he has some fey ability."

"He claims he does. He must or how else can he contact me? He remembers our past lives together. When he tells me about them, I seem to remember parts. He told me because I have worked so hard to forget some things that I have forgotten him, too. He seems like such a kind, gentle man. When he speaks in my head, I almost feel like everything is right in the world. When he leaves my mind, I feel like something is missing." Her fingers strayed to her forehead. Where was Clayton now? Perhaps he was asleep.

"Ahh, I can tell by your voice you like this man. Did you say you hear his voice in your head? How often?"

She did like him, not that she had thought about it all that much. She tried not to. It would be just her luck to fall for someone in the past once she'd decided she could have a regular life that could include love and possibly a family. "I do like him. It's hard to explain, but I feel I can be myself with him. I don't have to hide anything, because he knows all my thoughts. He knows who I am and loves me anyway."

Grandpa snorted into the phone before speaking. "Who wouldn't love you? You're damn near perfect, beautiful, intelligent, kind, and a promising healer."

His fierceness at lauding her virtues made her laugh. "Grandpa, you are supposed to think those things because we're related."

"It doesn't mean they're not true." His voice sank into a gravelly grumble.

Nora laughed again. "I'll take any compliments I can get, but trust me, not all those around me see me the way you do."

"They're fools then, not worth your time. I am more curious about this Clayton. Tell me more about him."

"Ah, well, um…" She hesitated in answering, blushing a little to say the words. "He thinks his life has no meaning without me by his side. That's why he searched for me. He didn't want to live out his life alone."

Grandpa muttered a few indistinct words Nora wasn't sure he meant her to hear. "Tell me. Is he so ugly no woman would want him? Without charm or humor, forcing him to pay for company?"

"Grandpa!" She was shocked that her own relative hinted the man might purchase companionship. She'd seen the girls advertising for dates not too far from their apartment. There was a spa down the street from them that she knew didn't specialize in neck and shoulder massages as stenciled on their windows. The steady stream of unsavory men patronizing it made both Tonya and Nora cross the street when they had to walk by.

"Clayton is very handsome and charming. He has a lovely Irish lilt and an intuitive knowledge that helps him understand what is wrong with people. He reminds me of you, in some ways."

"Go pulling that last bit on me and I'm forced to like him, but it sounds to me as if you are half in love with him."

"Yes." A sob bubbled up in her throat as she pushed the word out. "What am I going to do?"

"What do you want to do?"

"Grandpa, that's why I called you. You're the time-travel expert. I want to be with him in his time, but on the other hand, I want to bring him here to mine. Tell me what has to happen so we can be together in one century."

His sigh carried over the phone and didn't bode well. "Sweetheart, I'm not sure I can help you. I discovered a portal somewhat by accident. I knew in that second I would have to go through to be there for Leah, who hadn't been born yet. You might find a portal and end up in a time and place you don't want to be. If you do find a way to reach Clayton, you might not be able to come back to your time or family. Think about that."

"That's a troubling detail. All I know is Clayton needs my help, and I want to be there for him."

"I will look into this for you. Try to figure out where Clayton is and what year, even day, it is. The two of you seem to have a more powerful bond than I have ever heard of. I could not reach your grandmother when I was in the past. I did try several times. Tonight, when you go to sleep try to bring up an image of Clayton. Perhaps this will allow the two of you to connect, and you can ask him the needed questions."

"I will. I love you."

"I'm not really happy about the idea of giving up my granddaughter when I just returned to this time. All the same, I will not stand in the way of soul mates. The years were endless without my beloved Esmeralda by my side. Be safe. Call me when anything comes up, night or day. I love you, too."

"Okay, Grandpa." She thumbed off the phone and sat, looking at it. What if her association with Clayton meant breaking with her family? She'd always thought that as an adult she'd grow away from them, not that she disliked them. She spent less time with them with college, her job, and classes. She could count on one hand how many times she'd been home in the past year.

Still, that was not the same as never seeing them, which is what would happen if she could go to Clayton's time. It would be much nicer if he came to hers, which was selfish of her, considering the people he was helping.

"Really, Goddess, you have to present me with the perfect man and put him in the wrong century?"

No help for it. With no answer on carried on the air or in her head, she might as well get ready for bed. Brushing her teeth, she imagined what her conversation with Brandon would be when she returned to work. First, she'd have to inquire if Ogden had talked to him. If he hadn't, there would be no need to have the conversation. If he had, then she'd simply explain she already had a guy. No need to add he was in another century. Nope, that wouldn't make her sound very credible. Guys probably didn't care for mentally unbalanced females. It would, however, be one way to keep Brandon at a distance. Most probably feared an unbalanced woman might go psycho and pull a knife. Groaning, she discarded the thought of pretending to be crazy almost as soon as it occurred.

Running a brush through her hair, she considered growing it out. Maybe it was time to claim the right to wear her hair any way she wanted without fear of it being used to restrain her. She tiptoed into the living room to check on Tonya. The afghan lay in a heap on the floor, indicating Tonya must have retired to her own bed.

It was time for her to sleep, as well. Did she want to dream of Clayton? She desired to be with him, near him, hear his voice, but now she fought uncertainty. Would being with the charming Irishman mean giving up all she knew? She didn't know. All she really knew was that she was tired, and sleep sounded excellent.

CHAPTER NINE

Nora stretched out on her thin mattress, twisting one way, then another, the metal frame protruding through the cheap padding poking her in the back or side whenever she rolled. The idea behind the futon had been that it could be a couch when not used as a bed. It had failed as a couch, too. After graduation and landing a job, her first big purchase would be a mattress that didn't torture her all night.

Exhaustion wrapped around her, making her joints ache and her eyes gritty. Still, sleep eluded her. Better put, she didn't dare sleep. What if she ended up in another century? Grandfather hadn't been as much help as she'd hoped in that department. He'd seemed to think she had to make a decision, suggesting if she made a decision to stay with Clayton, then somehow she'd end up with him.

Wow, didn't she even get to go out for coffee a few times with the man before committing to his century? She wanted to see Clayton and explore this feeling between them. Life without Laundromats and cell phones didn't hold too much appeal.

Rotating her body diagonally, she located a spot without a bar. Closing her eyes, she imagined a white light cocooning her, a veil of protection. She remembered Nana teaching her the visualization when she'd been afraid of the neighbor's dog. The chained dog had often lunged and snarled at her when she walked by, and she'd feared it would break free and have her for breakfast. The protection spell had helped relieve her anxiety, and eventually the neighbor moved.

Exhaustion pinned her arms and legs to the bed, and she slipped into the corridor between awareness and sleep. She felt the final tumble into sleep almost as if she were in a boat and pushing off from shore. How pleased her English professor, Dr. Hadley, would have been with the imagery. He despaired of getting anything creative out of medical students.

She drifted in a fog of sorts. Nana called it lucid dreaming when awareness allowed you to take control in your dreams. People chased by animals or monsters could turn and tell them to stop chasing them. People dreaming of their own death could resurrect their lifeless body.

The white mist swirled about her, obscuring everything as she walked, but voices still penetrated. Soft, muted voices, as if she were listening through a wall. Nothing sounded familiar, but she did notice they altered as she walked. What was the place she was in? It wasn't frightening, but she had never been there before. Maybe the mist was the white light of protection she had wrapped around herself.

Clayton's voice came through clearly. "I need some help here."

Nora burst into a jog, moving toward the voice coming from in front of her. Breaking through a heavy cloud, she entered a clearing where a fire burned. Behind it, a large building had the doors flung open. The smell of vomit and decay rode the air. Her nose crinkled at the stink. A rough-looking Clayton appeared in the doorway with beard-shadowed face and stained clothing. His eyes showed his relief.

"Thank goodness, you heard my call."

Her eyes took in the high-noon sun as she approached the weary healer. Hours were different as you traveled through time.

"What's happening?" She could see rows of pallets holding moaning occupants inside the building. One woman, garbed in a long dress and apron, went from person to person, offering sips of water from the same ladle.

Clayton reached Nora in two long-legged steps and grasped her hands tightly. "I knew you would come."

Her eyebrows arched on their own, since she'd had no intention of coming, not that she was willing to confess that. The fire flared and sputtered behind her, drawing her attention. "Are you burning something or sterilizing?"

"Both. I have some general utensils in a pot near the edge. I am burning all the clothing and bedding to prevent contamination." He let go of her hands and stepped closer to the pot.

Nora clamped down on her bottom lip, unsure if she should point out that, the people were sharing the same water dipper, which went back into the water, mingling germs. The last person to drink would have a germ-laced cocktail and would probably be the first to succumb.

The helpful nurse eased a child into a seated position to help him drink.

Pointing to the child, Nora asked, "How healthy is that child?"

Rubbing his hand over his face, Clayton's expression remained tired. "Ahh." He shook his head before continuing. "Little Jimmy should be well by now. He shows signs of getting better, but then he takes another downturn. I know the boy. He was a healthy ten-year-old until his little sister contracted the illness."

She nodded as she listened. "It's probably because he is getting a fresh exposure to the illness every day."

Sweat beaded on her upper lip and brow from the heat. Here she stood in pajama pants and T-shirt, and perspiration dampened her clothes. How much worse was it for those inside? "All the germs are circulating in the air inside the building. The sickness stays inside, re-infecting those who could get well. If that isn't enough"—she indicated the ladle-wielding matron—"on her errand of mercy, she is gathering the germs of all and serving them up in a dipper of water."

Clayton's eyes grew larger as she watched the woman. "Margaret, could you bring me the bucket and the dipper?"

The woman looked up in surprise and nodded. She carried the bucket over and set it near Clayton, giving Nora a curious stare in the process.

Feeling the woman's scrutiny, she fingered her soft pajama pants. "What am I wearing?"

Did others see her? Maybe only Clayton saw her, but the woman did appear to be staring at her.

Clayton tipped out the water and allowed it to drain into the dry ground. He carried the bucket to the kettle of boiling water and dipped it in. He turned back to Nora and allowed his eyes to roam over from her head to her feet and back again. Only, on the second review, his eyes seemed to get stuck at breast level. Oh, great, she wasn't wearing a bra. Plucking her shirt away from her breasts, she managed to break the man's sudden absorption.

Shaking his head, he managed a sheepish grin. "Your costume is a top and pants decorated with a smiling cat." He stepped closer to rub fabric between his fingers. "It is soft."

His actions caused her to sweat a little more. It had to be the fire, until he whispered into her ear, "I believe you aren't wearing any undergarments."

She gave him a hard shove that only made him laugh. Clayton, while speaking the truth, was only teasing her. If any other man had said that to her, it would have seemed a threat, a prelude to a possible rape.

"Nora, my dear, what do we do about the drinking water?" He kept his distance, perhaps aware he might have overstepped his bounds.

She recognized what he was doing with the change in subject. Men across time were similar in some ways. Ah, yes, the water, she had an easy answer for that. "I think the safest thing to do would be to use individual cups. Each person could have a cup only for personal use. Clean water could be dipped into that."

Clayton pushed back the lock of wayward hair dipping toward his eyes with an impatient push of his fingers. "That we can do. What other words of wisdom do you have from the future for me?"

Words of wisdom from the future. Was the man mocking her? He didn't look like it. No smart-aleck smirk, no crossed arms, just a bone-weary man trying to do the job of a dozen people. "What are the symptoms? Have you had any fatalities?"

His eyes rolled up as he thought. "Well, before I got here, Granny Wagner passed, along with the Timmons' youngest. Most of the folks display weakness, fever, vomiting, general aches and pains, some coughing, stuffy noses, and runs. What do you think it is?"

The symptoms were rather flu-like and could indicate almost anything from the flu to typhoid. Lack of modern sanitation methods was the culprit with typhoid spreading, which was true with cholera, too. Cholera was a problem throughout the time until last century, her century. "Do you know if the water the population uses is possibly contaminated with fecal matter from humans or livestock?"

His brow furrowed as he considered the possibility. "This is a fairly dry area. Most people use deep wells. People use a few streams for livestock. Could be they might draw from the stream the livestock use." His hand scrubbed over his beard a few times before he continued speaking.

"Most folks know enough to get water from the springs. Imagine a lad told to fetch water might dip his bucket in whatever body of water was closest."

Nora found herself nodding in agreement. "Cholera is only one possibility. Has there been any news of outbreaks near here?"

She glanced around the dusty town, looking for any sign of life. A few women stood outside a building and stared in her direction, even shading their eyes to get a better look. Better chance they were looking at Clayton, still gorgeous despite the stubble and the mixed scent of sweat, sickness, and the musky masculine note. They weren't close enough to smell him, but she doubted they'd mind. Angling her head at the women, she commented, "Do you think my Hello Kitty pajamas are causing outrage among the populace?"

Clayton gave her another casual once-over, starting at her feet, but his eyes snagged again right at the cat's eyes on her shirt. He jerked his head up. "You'll be needing to change. Rose might have something you can wear. I'll not have the men, even if the sick ones, looking at my betrothed in such scandalous attire."

Placing both hands on her hips, which only seemed to tighten her shirt, she protested his remark. "Hey, I'm decent. All covered up, only my feet and arms showing."

"Too much for this century," Clayton grumbled as he headed to the building that housed the sick. "Rose."

It might have been helpful to know time-wise where she was. "What century is it?"

Not stopping his stride, he threw the words over his shoulder, "The nineteenth, of course."

Jogging after him, she stepped on a stone, causing her to curse and hop about on one foot. Clayton stopped, turned, and dropped to one knee, taking her abused foot in his hand. Nora balanced herself by placing her hand on his shoulder.

His thumb rubbed over her bruised instep, causing a twinge of residual pain, but the simple touch sent a flicker of electricity through her similar to the time she'd touched a frayed lamp cord. The man had chemistry to spare and then some.

"Aye, another reason to wear shoes. A lass doesn't show her feet off to anyone, except her intended. Seeing that it is me doing the seeing, there is no scandal in it."

He glanced up and speared her with a look from his heavily lashed eyes. Her knees weakened at the desire she read there. If a man could brand her with a simple glance, then she stood well marked.

Her fingers tightened on his shoulders to keep herself upright. Difficult, considering the man still held her foot. Pulling it back a little, she signaled him to release his hold. Her foot touched the ground, and she shifted her weight to get her balance. Even though she was hesitant to release his shoulder, there was no way he could kneel at her feet all day.

A pair of birds trilled overhead, interrupting the moment. There was an epidemic to investigate and stop.

Clayton stood, brushed off his knee, and gave her a slow, promising smile. Then, as if remembering what he was about, he turned again toward the building, calling out to the mysterious Rose. "I need a favor."

Watching the ground carefully for other painful rocks, Nora scampered after Clayton, touching his elbow. "Um, I have a question about what you just said."

He grinned at her, and then turned his head toward a woman coming his way. Nora took in the shapely woman, who had red curls and wore a colorful dress half-hidden by an oversized apron. As she came closer, Nora realized the woman sported makeup, a lot of it.

When she was about a foot away from Clayton, her eyes roamed over him in obvious appreciation. "What can I do for my favorite Irishman?"

The woman's words grated and Nora's spine stiffened with dislike at how the woman talked to her intended. She'd been about to complain about all his references to her being his betrothed and soul mate, but never mind.

A cloud of rose-scented perfume floated around the beauteous Rose. Nora coughed, choking on the strong scent, drawing attention to herself.

The woman appeared surprised. Hadn't she seen Nora standing a foot away from Clayton? At one time, Nora's goal had been to be ignored. Who knew she succeeded so well?

Clayton grinned in her direction and took a step closer to her, which pleased her very much. Might as well let Miss Heavily Made-Up Rose know where things stood.

"Nora, my darling, came to my aid without a stitch of clothing to her name."

Who was he calling my darling? It had better well be her. The surge of possessiveness—or was it jealousy?—had never shown up before. Then again, she'd never really ever had anything someone else wanted.

The look Rose shot her did nothing to relieve her jealousy. The woman gave her a snarky look similar to a few she'd encountered from the nurses at the hospital. "I see." She managed to wrap the two words with a heavy layer of contempt.

"Yes, I was wondering if you might have a dress, or even shoes, to lend our visiting healer. I'd count it as a favor, if you did." Clayton's hopeful expression cinched the deal.

Rose managed to inflict one more disdainful look at Nora's attire before answering. "I'd do anything for you, darling." Using her red-taloned hand, she gave Clayton's chest a pat. "Remember your offer. I'll collect on the favor."

Nora's hands fisted. Rose would not collect on the favor if she could help it. Pictures of the redhead entwined around Clayton had her wanting to punch the woman, or at least give her a satisfying push.

Unaware of Nora's desire to do serious damage to her smooth face, Rose said, "Follow me. I am sure I can find you something more appropriate to wear." The redhead turned and walked away with hips swinging, aware that people would be watching.

Nora moved directly behind her, blocking the effect of the show. If she ever tried to walk in that manner, she'd probably knock her hip out of joint. Her roommate, Tonya, would laugh herself to death first.

An embellished sign hung from the porch Rose mounted. Nora picked out the words between the fancy lettering and decorative flourishes. It certainly was fancier than the building she'd just left. She read the words aloud, "Heart of the Rose Gentleman Parlor and Saloon."

Rose opened the front door and half-turned to see if she was following.

"What is a gentleman parlor?" Nora asked.

A black-haired woman with a general air of weariness and attired only in a scarlet poppy robe walked toward them. "Well, where did you find this one? She must be green if she has no clue that 'gentleman parlor' is a genteel way of saying whorehouse."

Aha, now she understood the overuse of makeup and the amazing hip swing. It was advertising.

Rose's eyebrows lifted as she considered the woman lounging against the bar. "Lydia, I have a job for you. Get the Irish healer's doxy dressed." She paused, as if considering her words. "Suited for ministering to the sick."

The women exchanged a look, which said more than their words. Lydia grabbed Nora's arm and tugged her along.

"I can walk." Nora jerked her arm out of the woman's grasp.

Lydia grumbled to herself, more than to Nora. "You speak English. With your chopped hair, tanned skin, and clothing, I figured you for an Indian or a half-breed, not a resident of the town of Dalton."

They passed a series of doors as Nora examined her skin. It wasn't all that dark, though it was darker than Rose's or Lydia's. "I am American, same as you. As for my hair, I chose to cut it. These are my sleeping clothes. I arrived unexpectedly without other clothing."

Lydia threw a knowing look over her shoulder. "Uh-huh, I can see how that might happen with a handsome, charming Irishman."

Nora started to protest the assumption, but what could she say? That she and Clayton were betrothed, or that she was from a different time, or maybe that the two of them had been a couple for the last seven hundred years or so? Each statement sounded worse than the last.

Lydia threw a door open and gestured for Nora to enter. Inside were clothes hanging on hooks and spilling out of boxes, shoes scattered around the floor. A rickety-looking dresser with half-closed drawers revealed stockings and corsets. "Looks like Imogene did a number on the wardrobe. A settler passing through asked her to be his wife. She must have ripped the place apart to find something matronly to wear."

Satin dresses that dripped with lace tempted Nora. Her fingers smoothed over a red dress bedecked with black trim, cheap perfume and body odor still clinging to the fabric. She never dressed alluring. Never had any reason to, just the opposite to play down her curves. All the same, she was still amazed at how much attention she received from men. Tonya blamed it on how she still had a pretty face and how men liked to unwrap packages.

Lydia turned with what looked like a long swatch of brown burlap. "This will do." She handed the fabric to Nora. Nora shook it out. It did resemble a dress somewhat, an ugly one. Bringing it up to her nose, she sniffed it. At least it didn't smell bad.

"Wait," the woman said before Nora could leave the room. "Dress won't do much good to dampen masculine interest if we don't tie those down." Her out-flung hand was at chest level. Her point was a valid one. She pulled out a corset and a chemise.

Nora eyed the corset and its many laces with disapproval. She wasn't a fan of a sports bra, and this looked like one for her entire body. Oh, well, if it was a dream, it shouldn't hurt. Still, shouldn't she get to wear what she chose in a dream? Brandishing the burlap dress, she shook it. "I don't like this dress. Why can't I wear something pretty?"

Shoving the drawer shut, Lydia turned and put both hands on her hips. "Lord have mercy, you are green. A claimed woman, that's what you are."

Nora was about to protest the designation, but the woman continued speaking, enlightening her. "It does not matter if you are married, hand-fasted, promised, or even just sparking. Once a man claims you, he does not want any man looking at ya.

The best way to discourage that is ugly clothing. Get dressed and let me see how it fits." Lydia shoved a pair of cotton socks at her already full hands.

Nora looked pointedly at Lydia, who turned her back to allow her some privacy.

The woman grumbled, "I have no clue how you are going to survive here in the West."

Pulling a chemise, more like a short slip, over her head, she muttered through the muslin material. "You and me both."

The corset baffled her with its many laces and hooks.

Lydia removed it from her hands and began loosening the ties. "It is best to never unlace it all the way because it will take forever to do up." She held out the widened undergarment. "Pull it over yer head. Then, I will lace you up. I cannot believe your mother never had you in a corset. Were you raised by heathens?"

Nora started to answer, "Pagans," but the tight squeeze of the laces cut off her breath. Working her hand under the corset, she managed to loosen it. "What do I wear underneath?"

She didn't expect any panties or thongs, but she expected something. Hadn't she read that they wore bloomers or something?

Lydia guided the dress over Nora's head. "Oh, you mean the drawers with the slit in them."

There was a slit in them? That was news to her. Although it made sense when the women had to deal with long skirts and corsets, the idea of walking around with a hole in her underwear was a bit unsettling.

"None here. As working girls, all that extra material just gets in the way." Lydia smoothed the material over Nora's back and buttoned up the dress. "It looks like it will fit you fine. That will make Rose mad."

There was a faint design in the material, and it didn't look as horrible on as she'd expected.

"Take a peek in the mirror while I hunt for giant shoes for your big feet."

Nora winced at the summation of her feet. She pulled up the hem of her dress to gaze at the body parts in question.

Before she knew it, Rose was guiding her back to Clayton with a less-than-pleased attitude. Maybe she did look good.

Clayton looked up from where he squatted beside a pallet, holding the hand of an elderly woman. "Who is this vision of loveliness that Rose is escorting?"

A blush crept into Nora's cheeks. The corset gave her an hourglass figure that threw both her hips and breasts into prominence. It wasn't something she'd wear all the time, but she was glad to look good for Clayton, especially when standing next to the showy Rose. A giggle bubbled up in her throat, making her sound like a teenager. Maybe it was to be expected, since she'd bypassed those teenage years without a boyfriend. She was starting rather late, but at least she was starting the romantic dance when only a few days before she'd never thought she would.

Rose gave her a little push as if she were a wayward child or a wandering cow. "Here she is. You can thank me later over at the parlor."

Call her green, but even she'd figured out what was going on at the parlor and what type of thanks Rose might want. The woman on the pallet blushed at Rose's bold words.

Clayton shook his head. "I'll be thanking you right here, Rose. A lovely job you've done with my intended. I had no doubts, because you had such a beauty to work with."

An angry flush mottled Rose's cheeks and exposed neck. Nora could tell the woman was not pleased to hear Clayton make his intentions clear.

Clayton looked back at the flushed woman. "Will you be volunteering with us anymore this day?"

Rose pivoted on her heel and walk swiftly away without answering or any extraneous hip movements.

The woman on the pallet whistled. "Thank ye. I am feeling better already what with seeing that tart handed her comeuppance. The woman stayed to make sure none of her regular customers died and to secure the attentions of your man. Good thing you showed up when you did."

"Good thing," Nora agreed, lifting an eyebrow at the man in question.

Placing his hand on his heart, he swore with his Irish accent growing thicker. "I am loyal to you throughout time."

There were many ways she could have replied to his declaration, but not in front of the dear, sweet, old lady. "Clayton, I was wondering if I might help your patient out of the building. Maybe to sit under a tree. With her doing so well, I'd hate for her to stay in such a germ-infested area."

Before Clayton could answer, the woman pushed herself up. "Name is Mary. Some call me Granny. Either would do. Come, help me out to that tree, and you can tell me all about your courtship."

Crouching, she helped Mary up and outside to sit underneath a spreading oak tree. "Tell me, Mary, do you live near a stream or use water from a stream?"

"Good heavens, no. My late husband, Jonah, drilled a deep well that has never run dry," the woman announced with a smile.

Helping the woman to sit with her back against the tree trunk, Nora considered discarding cholera as the possible cause for the illness. The woman held her hand and urged her to sit, a bit against her will, since she was eager to return and help Clayton. Wasn't she in control of her dream? Resting her back against the tree, she realized Mary had the same spunkiness as her own grandmother.

"Tell me about your beau. Most people do not have any use for the Irish, but I can tell your man is different. Was it love at first sight?"

That would depend on when she'd first met him. Apparently, she hadn't fallen for him immediately the first time or the second. "The first time I saw him, this year," she clarified to separate this time from all the previous lifetimes they'd shared, "I was surprised because I didn't expect someone like him, and yet I felt as if I knew him."

Mary cackled with glee and slapped Nora's leg, demonstrating her much-improved health. A bird trilled with the woman as if it were laughing too.

CHAPTER TEN

The birdcall morphed into an alarm waking Nora. A hammering began on the door. "Shut that stupid alarm off." The door popped open under persistent knocking, and Tonya stumbled into the room, grabbing on to the open door for balance.

Nora pushed herself up, her ribs hurting, to see her roommate looking at her in horror. She fingered the offending area only to discover a covering equivalent to the compression bandages used on burn victims.

Tonya swayed a bit while using the door as an anchor. Releasing her grip, she stumbled a few steps and fell onto the bed. Grabbing the long skirt, she held it up, rubbing the material through her fingers. "It's real."

Nora looked at the dress in bewilderment. It was what she'd worn in her dream. Was this part of her dream? Touching Tonya, she asked, "Are you part of my dream?"

Tonya pinched her hand.

"Ouch!" She jerked her abused hand away from sharp fingernails. "Why did you do that?"

Tonya sighed. "Do you miss the obvious? I had to see if you were dreaming."

Nora eased herself close enough to twist a good chunk of caramel-colored skin on Tonya's arm.

"Hey, that hurts. What was that all about?" Tonya complained and scooted out of pinching range.

"I'm sorry. I was just checking to see if you were dreaming."

"If I were dreaming, my head wouldn't hurt so much. What I can't figure out is what you are wearing. You aren't into some of those kinky role-playing games, are you? If you are, then who are you playing with?" Tonya pushed up the hem of Nora's dress to expose the rough work boots Lydia had finally located for her. "Those are some butt-ugly boots."

Nora tugged her skirt away from her friend's fingers. "Help me get out of these clothes. There is no way I can do it on my own." She turned to present her back.

Once the tiny buttons came loose, the top of the dress sagged, and her roommate's voice carried a tone of amazement. "I'll be damned. Is this one of those *Gone with the Wind* corsets?"

"I just want it gone. It is squeezing me." Nora wiggled her shoulders and tried to draw in a deep breath, but failed. "I can't even breathe in this contraption."

Tonya slid off the bed. "Stand up, this thing seems to go on forever. Who put it on you?"

The eased laces allowed her to breathe a little deeper. She swallowed the reminder not to unlace the corset all the way to make it easier to lace up again later. No way was it going back on. It felt as if it had left permanent grooves in her skin. "Oh, Lydia put it on me. If I'd had any clue what it would feel like, I would have axed the idea."

Tonya grunted and pulled at a tangled section. "Would you object if I got a knife and cut this off you?"

Nora followed her to the kitchen, where Tonya located a knife and carefully sawed away at the laces. The offending corset dropped to the floor, allowing Nora to breathe again. She stepped out of the corset and slid the dress from her body, leaving her in a chemise, petticoats, and work boots.

"You look like something from those steampunk illustrations. Tell me about your playmate, Lydia. Personally, I didn't think you swung that way, but on meeting Ogden, I could understand if you don't go for men." Tonya opened the fridge to search for something edible.

Placing both hands on her hips, Nora talked to Tonya's back. "I do, too, like men. I even have a charming Irishman to call my own."

Tonya straightened too fast, hitting her head on the fridge. "Woman, you are killing me." Resting against the counter, she retrieved a bag of peas from the freezer and held it against her head. "What crazy shit have you got mixed up in?"

Picking up the corset, Nora held it out for a friend's inspection. "Look at it carefully. This is no fancy lingerie. It's the real thing. Over a hundred years old, maybe more. A saloon girl in the tiny town of Dalton gave it to me to wear. Showing up in my Hello Kitty pajamas was not acceptable."

Tonya put up one hand. "Stop, let me at least sit down." Holding the frozen peas in place, she pulled a chair out from the table. She eased down as not to jar her head. "Go ahead."

Nora pulled out another chair and bent to unlace her heavy boots, talking from her upside-down position. "I met my soul mate, but he isn't in this century. He's a sexy Irishman with eyes I can lose myself in. Strong arms to hold me tight. He has this great curly hair that is always falling into his eyes."

"Okay. Enough. You convinced me you're still hetero. When do you have time to meet this sexy beast of a man with school, clinical, work, and the ever-obnoxious Ogden?" Tonya lowered the peas and placed them on the table.

Boots off, Nora peeled off her socks before sitting up to face her friend. It would be hard to explain, but she needed to try. "I meet him while I'm asleep. He came looking for me across the centuries because we've been soul mates forever."

Tonya blinked a couple of times and then pushed out of the chair. "I think I need caffeine to understand what you're saying."

Nora stood up, too, wiggling her bare toes against the floor. Who would want to wear such heavy footwear? "Tonya, I know you believe in reincarnation. With that being the case, why can't you accept that I've met my soul mate from several past lives?"

Her friend stood with a can of coffee in one hand and the measuring cup in the other. "I believe in reincarnation in theory, just like some people believe in heaven, and those religion nut jobs who think they are going to get their own planet and those other religions that say there is going to be an Armageddon. It is only a theory. No one has seen any of this stuff. We might like to believe it, but we have no proof it is real."

"Look at me. I'm your proof. Remember the other morning when I woke smelling like wood smoke?" Nora held her arms out, not knowing how she could explain time travel or past lives when she didn't understand them herself.

"What's that smell?" Tonya's nose crinkled as if offended. She began to search the room while Nora sniffed herself.

"I will admit to some body odor. I'll take a shower. It was really hot in Dalton." She shrugged her shoulders apologetically.

Her friend's lips formed a mulish line. "That isn't it. It's a familiar aroma from my childhood."

"Does it smell like the sea? Fish? Coconut? Shrimp on the barbie?" Nora questioned, watching her friend pick up a discarded sock and sniff it.

Tonya threw her a long-suffering glare. "I am from Jamaica, not Outback Steakhouse." She picked up the ugly boots and turned them over. "Bingo. Horse shit. Now I believe you."

"Why do you believe me now? I've come back in period clothes, down to some torture-device underwear, but horse manure convinces you?" She threw her hands in the air in frustration, but was secretly glad that someone outside of her grandfather did believe her.

Tonya laughed at her frustration. "I will tell you. First, this is a mixture of manure. Old, new, different horses. Trust me, when you had to clean out the stables every day, you get good at recognizing the smells. We are in the middle of the city. I can't even think where you would go that had horses. Even if there was somewhere within a thirty-mile range, I doubt they'd let you come in at the dead of night dressed in period costume to stomp around their fields or stables. Now that makes sense. More sense than someone loving you over centuries does. Do you think you just might be lonely?"

Why could her friend accept involuntary time travel, but not the fact someone had loved her for centuries? "Of course, I'm lonely. I have been lonely all my life. I didn't realize what was missing until I met Clayton. He's my other half."

Tonya placed her hand on Nora's forehead as if feeling for a fever. "Girlfriend, you are starting to sound like one of those teen novels. Did you forget we are grown-ass women? We don't need no man to make things work."

Nora rolled her eyes, trying to keep her temper in check. She had so few friends she could not afford to offend any. "That may be true, but it doesn't stop me from wanting to be part of a couple or having someone to love. Clayton is that man. If you met him, then you'd know. You'd see it."

Wagging a finger, her friend exclaimed, "Don't be calling me closed-minded. I see it in your face. Show me this great love of your life, and I'll make up my mind."

Her blood pressure shot up with her anger. Why couldn't she get her friend to believe her? "I will get him here. I will introduce him to you. You'll see." She stomped off to the shower, as well as one can stomp barefoot and in a period petticoat.

Turning on the shower, she realized she had traveled back to his time. But how could she bring her man to the twenty-first century when didn't know how she'd done it? Life certainly would be easier if they could be together in the same time. They could scrape together something that resembled a normal dating relationship. Shedding her chemise and petticoats, she stepped into the shower. Had she even helped when she'd returned to Clayton's time?

Squeezing the shampoo, she managed a healthy dollop for her time-ravaged hair. No doubt, it smelled as bad too. Hair lathered up and suds running into her eyes, she stepped under the warm stream of water at the same time that Clayton spoke.

You were a mighty help, darling.

Her automatic response was to try to cover her breasts and lady parts with her hands. Unfortunately, she was short one hand. A chuckle reverberated in her head.

I am not able to see anything. More's the pity.

Nora wondered if he was telling the truth as she rinsed the shampoo out of her hair. It was good having him with her. It would give them a chance to discuss the epidemic. Bending, she picked up the conditioner and flipped up the lid with her thumb.

You doubt my honesty? I am hurt. Use your mind. There's no reason you can't read me as easily as I read you.

The thought intrigued her but somehow seemed wrong. Leah had explained when she'd slipped into the past that she'd had the ability to read minds, but that ability had slipped away with Leah's return. Just as well, since Nora didn't really want to know what some people were thinking.

I know your thoughts, lass, because we are one. I thought if you knew my own heart was set on only you, perhaps that might relieve you.

Maybe. I guess in a way I am reaching your mind already since we are conversing.

She picked up the body pouf and wondered if he really couldn't see her. The bath gel scent filled the shower with the heady aroma of blackberries.

Clayton, can you tell me what I am doing now?

I cannot see you. Your mind speaks of bathing in blackberries. This I don't understand. Milk baths, yes. Blackberries, no. Does it not stain your skin?

Nora laughed, imagining a tub of berries. *My soap only smells like blackberries. Tell me about the people of Dalton. Are they improving?*

Dalton's crisis has passed. Rains came. They washed away the germs, fears, and horrible heat. You were right about sharing the water. Once we used different cups, the sick became better faster. I cautioned people about using the streams. In fact, I left Dalton more than a week ago.

Nora stopped in mid-motion of drying herself. *I was just there last night.*

No, my love, it was more than a week ago.

How could that be? Time definitely wasn't linear. Einstein had expressed the idea that time was stacked on top of each other rather like an unrolled ribbon. The time continuum must not line up day by day. *To me, it was last night.*

Trust me, darling, it was a week. A long, lonely week without you.

Nora's lips tipped up, imagining Clayton's eyes twinkling as he spoke the words. He did miss her. That she knew to be true. It made sense, because she missed him every minute they were apart.

Does my heart good to hear you say so.

Wrapping the towel around her body, she picked up her toothbrush. *That last part I didn't mean for you to hear.*

Perhaps you did. Could be you wanted to give my old heart some ease. I thank you for it. Oh, wait, someone is calling me. I'll be back when I can.

Just like that, he winked out right after she brushed her molars, but before she got to her bicuspids. She sighed, wondering if they'd ever shared a space for more than a day. Did she astral project? The fact she came home in different clothes meant she'd had a physical body. It shot down the idea of astral projection, because only your soul or essence traveled with none being the wiser.

Someone had to know more about this than she did. Toweling her hair dry, she made plans to visit the metaphysical bookstore near the university. College towns were fertile ground for eclectic stores that stretched the boundaries of accepted thought. Both she and Tonya had visited to buy herbs and charm candles. Most of their business probably came for spell supplies and Tarot readings. An older man helped the owner by photographing auras and did past-life readings. She wasn't sure how he was related to the owner, but he was usually there, manning the cash register or the aura camera.

Tonya had persuaded her one day to have her aura photographed. That had been a mistake. She kept her secrets close, but the camera had exposed them. The white-haired gentleman had explained their photos separately. Tonya's showed strength with the orange and flashes of turquoise. However, Nora's photo had disappointed her. There had been a white cloud over the green and yellow colors, making them hard to see. The cloud represented a barrier or block masking, making it difficult for some of her natural abilities to shine. While she hadn't liked the photographer's interpretation, she couldn't have said it was untrue. He'd be the perfect person to talk to about past lives and slipping in and out of centuries.

Her phone rang before she could leave the apartment. The temptation was to let it ring. No good would come from her answering it. It could be Ogden, ready to forgive her attitude if she'd just run a few errands for him. More likely, it was Barb wanting her to come in and work. The swing-shift cook who was supposed to replace each cook two times a week wasn't working out that well. Bonnie called him a crybaby because he complained about not having a normal life with a swing schedule. She thumbed her phone and held it to her ear only to hear Barb's voice.

"Oh, good, I was hoping to reach you."

Nora hadn't said a word. Maybe if she didn't respond, her boss might think she had the wrong number. The apartment was quiet. Maybe she'd think it was a dropped call. Besides, she was tired. Who knew how much sleep she'd managed to grab last night? It sure didn't feel like much. She dug her knuckle into her gritty left eye.

Tonya yelled from kitchen, "Was that your phone or mine?"

Busted. No way, Barb didn't hear that. She cleared her throat. "Oh, hello, Barb."

Her boss chose not to mention her earlier silence, but instead started her plea. "I need you to come in for second shift."

Nora's responsible part mentally agreed to work. After all, she could use the money. The other part, the one that had stayed up most of the night talking to dance-hall girls and a handsome healer, emphatically vetoed the idea. "Well, Barb, this is my first day off in an eight day stretch."

Saying no was not something she did well, which explained all the endless errands she'd performed for Ogden. Sometimes it seemed easier to agree than to explain why she logically couldn't do something. Today, she wasn't going into work, no way, no how.

"I know, I know. I wouldn't ask, but Doug called and asked me if he could be off."

Nora snorted her response, realizing too late that one should not snort at her boss.

"Hear me out. His little girl is sick. She's only two. It's touch-and-go. He needs to be by her side." Barb finished the words in the rush.

It all sounded over-the-top. Since they'd hired Doug, the man was off more than he worked, but if his little girl was sick, wouldn't she feel terrible if she refused to work? Still, she was willing to bet it was a far-fetched tale to get out of work. Bonnie would know the truth. The woman should work for the FBI. All it took was one look at her amazing cleavage and men would babble secrets they'd held for years.

Biting her bottom lip, Nora knew what she was going to do. "Okay, I'll be in at two. Maybe a little after. I have some errands to run. Is Ernie good with that?"

Barb's voice suddenly became cheerier. "Yes, yes, Ernie is great with that. You'll have to work only six hours since Brandon agreed to come in earlier. Bye."

Of course, Ernie would get orders as to what he'd do. He was already there. Barb had had to sweet-talk her. Apparently, she'd already called Brandon. But it would have been unreasonable to expect a cook to work back-to-back shifts. Maybe her boss had made up the story about Doug's daughter. Working would cut into her bookstore time.

"Tonya, I am heading out to Spiritual Dimensions. Do you want to come?"

It would be nice to have someone with her because the store's neighborhood was on the rough side, which explained the bars on the windows. The shop owners trusted in cold hard steel as opposed to amulets and charms. Nana had always warned her it was stupid not to use all your options. Bars represented another form of protection.

Her roommate held on to the bedroom door. "You go on. I need to rest. Captain Morgan is having a knock-down fight with the coffee. I think I am going to eat something to settle my stomach." She placed a hand over her stomach as if she expected something to jump out of it.

The definite greenish undertone of her skin kept Nora from mentioning how she felt about Tonya's helpful comment about Brandon. Her roommate was feeling bad enough. No reason for Nora to add to her misery.

"See ya in a couple of hours." She pulled the door closed with as little noise as possible.

CHAPTER ELEVEN

The bus was less crowded than usual, but then again she was heading to a section of town most people avoided. The good news was Spiritual Dimensions had a bus stop close to the shop. She pulled her amulet out from under her shirt to make sure it was on prominent display. There was usually a variety of aimless males roaming Division Street where the small shop sat. The cleaner, better-groomed males might be heading for the temporary office, which provided a variety of day labor positions. Nora never worried about them. It was the others, the ones who grabbed their groins while making kissy sounds in her direction, who scared her.

She was supposed to find that attractive? It equally repulsed and frightened her. Last time, Tonya had come with her. When one male had had the nerve to approach them, her friend had turned around so fast Nora almost got whiplash from avoiding her outstretched arm as she threw some magickal sand in the man's face, accompanied by a few unfamiliar words.

The man had actually run away, yelling about witches and spells. Tonya had reminded her that many ignorant people feared witches.

With that in mind, Nora hoped her exposed amulet of protection, along with the pentacle she donned at the last minute would serve as her own shield.

The streets looked relatively clear, probably due to the locals sleeping off the night before. Her stop was coming up. An elderly woman pushed up out of her seat to stand beside Nora to wait for the doors to open. Catching sight of her necklace, the woman fixed her gaze on it as if caught in some hypnotic trance. The woman stumbled back a couple of feet, as if Nora could zap her with an evil look.

Well, the pentacle still worked with the uninformed. Normally, she might have tried to explain that it had sentimental value, but not today. Too much to get done before she headed in for her extra shift. She did not feel up to dealing with prejudiced people who believed all the nonsense the church made up centuries ago about witches killing babies and drinking their blood. Thousands died as a result, some actual witches, though most only had the misfortune to cross someone in power. The church made it easy to wipe out the competition. The same type of ignorance made the skittish woman on the bus act as if Nora were some sort of demon.

Whenever she thought about the Burning Times and the thousands who had died, she became almost as incensed as Nana did, especially considering her little sister almost met a similar end.

A stubbly faced man shambled in her direction with one hand clutching his baggy pants but still exposing most of his dollar-sign boxers. Great. He'd either hit her up for a dollar or pretend to stumble to cop a feel.

Her fingers fisted around the amulet Nana had given her before she left for college. She mentally projected a thought—*don't come any closer*—surprised when he stumbled to a stop.

Casting one last look at the stunned man who stared straight in front of him as if he'd hit a brick wall, she began to jog to the shop. Why press matters? Who knew how long he'd remain that way? Her fingers ran across the cool metal and polished stones of the amulet. At one time, she'd believed in charms, amulets, and protection spells. Nothing, including the pentacle she wore then, had saved her from the attack. She was never sure why. Had the magick not been strong enough? Had her belief not been enough to power the charms? Maybe the combined evil of the players had overwhelmed any protection. She would never know.

After that, magick had become something her family did. Even though she'd witnessed it bringing Grandpa and Leah back from the past, it hadn't really seemed to touch her. Nora did, however, still celebrate the sabbats with Tonya, which knitted the two of them closer together. Last time they'd been at the bookstore, Tonya had wanted red charm candles for love spells.

A woman left the shop and nodded in Nora's direction. Her lips tried for a smile, but failed too got up in the remembrances of her previous visit. Had Tonya found a man after her love spells? Nora had sat with her and chanted, not expecting any results from the spells for herself. After all, she never expected love. The dreams had grown stronger after that, though. Before, she'd had a sense of dreaming, but that was all. After the spell, she'd remembered Clayton's eyes, if nothing else. They were always so welcoming.

An elderly man met her at the door with a smile. "She's here, Martha."

A woman with gray-streaked hair came through the curtains separating the store from the reading rooms. She looked relieved as she hurried toward Nora and reached for her hands. "Praise the Goddess, you've arrived. We have much to discuss." Still holding Nora's hands, she attempted to guide her to the back.

Nora stood her ground. She'd come to see the man to find out about her past lives. It was odd this woman was expecting her. Her eyes flickered to the hands still grasping hers.

"Don't worry, sweetie. We'll close the shop. Owen, lock the door. That way, we can both sit in on the reading."

The soothing recorded sounds of a rushing stream and birdcalls failed to counteract the effect of the woman's words. A quick glance around the store showed no one in the book aisles or hovering near the candle and oil counter. Could Martha and Owen really have meant her? Her first impression was that they couldn't have, but the nagging sense of unease during the past week had made her nervous, too. "I think you have mistaken me for someone else."

Martha tightened the blue-veined hands grasping Nora's. "I wish I were, child. The good news is we reached you before the evil did."

Before the evil did. That sounds ominous.

Nora inhaled briefly. Were all the Carpenter women doomed to have close encounters with evil? Why couldn't she live an ordinary life? Of course, who was to say her life wasn't ordinary? Not everyone confessed online everything that ever happened in his or her lives, despite the general impression.

Owen turned over the closed sign and switched off the neon lightning that read TAROT READINGS. He turned the lock and attempted to smile, but it didn't reach his eyes. The three of them turned to the backroom without a word.

The benevolence of Martha and Owen was evident in their faces and manners. If Nora had been anywhere else, she might have wondered about the intentions of an old couple herding her to the back of their store. Ironically, some non-pagans would have believed the two were up to nefarious purposes, from drinking her blood to harvesting her organs.

Martha pushed aside the curtain to reveal a small room crowded with a folding table decorated with a purple triquetra altar cloth featuring three interlocking ovals. Most people called the symbol the Celtic knot, and a few mistakenly tried to associate its origin with Christianity. Nora recognized it as the triple goddess emblem of the maiden, mother, and crone.

A pack of dog-eared Tarot cards sat on the table beside a dark scrying mirror. Three metal folding chairs sat scattered around the room, as if the previous occupants had left in a rush after getting bad news. Good chance she'd receive the same. Would she run from the store, too?

Not before the bus came. She knew that much. The store's neighborhood held enough real menace to keep her within the stone walls.

Owen offered her a chair with a gentlemanly flare that reminded her of Grandfather Buell. Martha placed a fat white candle in the center of the table for protection. The woman nodded at Owen, who began to walk the circle, scattering salt. It must be serious if they were resorting to salt.

At her family rituals, Nana usually created a protective circle with only mental energy. If her mother was feeling seasonal, flower petals or even seeds could serve as a barrier. Salt was for the serious stuff. It kept out entities and spirits that might prevent the ritual or possibly do the participants harm. Surely the store was protected, as stocked full of charms as it was. No doubt, the couple did a smudging ceremony each day before opening for business. Nana believed in smudging the house once a month to cleanse it of any negative energy. Her grandmother clutching the smoking stick of sage and waving it over Nora's crib was one of her earliest memories. The acrid aroma symbolized safety to her. Her nostrils flared as she tried to differentiate the lingering scent. The spicy smell was a familiar one, but definitely not sage.

It was sandalwood. That made sense, since it promoted visions and spirituality and opened the third eye. Maybe Martha had used it earlier after seeing something that alarmed her.

Owen finished creating a tight circle around the table, leaving a thick trail of salt. Nora glanced at the worn deck of cards, expecting the woman to pick them up. Instead, she lighted the white candle and withdrew a box from under the table. Polished stones of different minerals and a few ragged, cut ones crowded the box. She identified the smooth black stone decorated with patches of white as snowflake obsidian. The brownish gold jasper and smoky quartz were both protection stones. Maybe they all were.

Martha pushed the box in her direction. "Take four."

Nora picked out a blue-colored stone, a yellow triangular one, a square one that looked almost like a crystal ice cube, and a smooth gray one that almost looked metallic.

The woman nodded in the direction of the stones lying on the table. "Hold them in your hands. I want you to concentrate on all that matters most to you in the world."

Placing two rocks in each hand, Nora fisted her hands. The triangular one's edges bit into her skin. All that matters to her? That should be easy. She expected to think of her family and career, maybe even Tonya. The image of a smiling Clayton came to mind and refused to budge to make room for any others. When had this one man become so important in her life? She hadn't really known him that long. Maybe a month at the most.

Seven lifetimes, my darling. Have you forgotten already?

Clayton's voice startled her. She hadn't been expecting it. She never knew what time of day it was in his century. Should he be sleeping? Maybe she only remembered his voice. Did anyone else hear him? A quick glance at Martha caught the woman with fingers crossed and head bowed, trying to reach the plane where she could foresee.

Owen looked amused and whispered, "How wonderful it must be to carry your sweetheart with you."

Nora started to protest that it was damn spooky, but then she reconsidered. "It is rather nice."

Martha's head jerked up, making Nora wonder if they would be scolded for whispering while she meditated. The woman's voice was deep and somber. "Give me the first stone."

Nora placed the ice-cube-shaped rock in Martha's palm while holding on to the other three.

The woman turned the stone around, intently looking at it as if she'd not seen it only minutes before. "Much magick and travel are attached to your family. You are not the first to travel into the past."

Nora's breath hitched. You'd think living in a talented Wiccan family she'd be used to those who could foresee, but it always surprised her. Martha was the genuine article, not that Nora had doubted her before. She just preferred that nothing bad would happen. With her own time-traveling romance, a co-worker who thought she wanted his body, an angry Ogden, and only a few months until graduation, she didn't need anything else happening.

Martha put the cube rock down and motioned for the next one. She accepted the blue one and held it up to the light. A slight, raspy chuckle escaped the woman's lips.

"Oh, my, he's a handsome one with his dark eyes and wavy hair. Irish in his current lifetime, a charmer for sure. Yes, you've been soul mates, but yet I have never heard of people connecting over centuries." She put the rock down and looked at the man. "Have you, Owen?"

The man looked thoughtful. He spoke to Nora, who still had one hand clenched around the remaining two rocks. "Once. It was a powerful love forged over many lifetimes. I believe you two have such a bond."

A powerful love forged over many lifetimes. Wow. All she really wanted was a man who would love her as she was. Apparently, she'd found a man who had done that repeatedly. The pull he had on her wasn't something new at all.

Owen angled his head in the direction of Martha's outstretched hand. Nora fingered the gray shiny rock then dropped it on the table. Her actions surprised her. Why hadn't she given it to the woman? It was rather rude of her. Either her hand or the rock had taken charge of its location.

Martha placed her fingers on the rock to pick it up then jerked her hand back with a high-pitched yelp. Owen lunged up and leaned over the table to pat the aged woman's hand. "Are you okay, dear?"

Inhaling deeply, the woman motioned for Owen to sit. "Sit, do not break the circle." She touched the rock with the side of her hand. "So much evil I cannot bear to hold it." Martha settled a pain-filled look on Nora.

Nora felt horrible that somehow she'd hurt the woman. "Is the evil in me?"

It had never occurred to her that she might carry evil in her. She'd certainly never forgiven those who'd harmed her. Often, she became inpatient with others. A few times, she had wanted to hurt people. The Wiccan Rede forbade hurting others. Of course, she'd never lain a hand on anyone, but she'd wanted to.

Martha continued to bat the stone around with the corner of her hand and winced each time the stone touched her skin. "Oh, no, it's not you, but someone you come in contact with on a regular basis. So much evil that even slight contact with this person has coated you with the stench of malice."

An unpleasant foreboding snaked up her spine. "Is it someone I know?" She mentally reviewed everyone she knew, trying to decide if any of them were capable of pure evil. Tonya would say Ogden was, but he'd never tried to deceive her into thinking he was something he wasn't, or had he?

"Perhaps. It is hard to say without a better reading." The woman placed her palm over the stone then let out a bloodcurdling scream.

Nora grabbed Martha's hand and pulled it away from the stone. A surge went through her, almost like an electrical current. For a second, she could see darkness and the intent to harm her. Letting go of Martha's hand, Nora sat abruptly. How could she be carrying all that residual evil around with her?

Martha sat back in her chair with her eyes closed, breathing heavily.

Good Goddess, Nora hoped she hadn't caused the woman to have a heart attack. Owen grasped the edge of the table with whitened fingers, trembling a little.

"Is she okay?" Nora asked, wanting reassurance that she hadn't harmed the kindly woman, but feeling Owen might need it more.

Owen shook his head. "I hope so. Never saw a reading as bad as yours. Heavy magick at work." He pointed to the amulet around her neck. "I bet you didn't buy that at a street festival."

Her fingers drifted up to grasp the necklace, which seemed to be warm and throbbed as if alive. "No, my nana gave it to me for protection."

Owen glanced at Martha whose eyes opened. She sat up straight and assumed a somber expression as if nothing had happened. "Your nana must be powerful, because the magick has kept you safe."

Thinking back on that one terror-filled night when the whole course of her life had changed, Nora almost said that it hadn't always kept her safe, but Nana hadn't yet bestowed this particular charm upon her.

As if reading her thoughts, Owen's weathered hand covered her empty hand. "I am sorry for the pain, but that one night changed you and set you on the path you needed to be. Not all evil is purely evil. Sometimes it teaches us something we need to learn or teaches others. It wouldn't be as wonderful as we think to have no pain in our lives."

Sucking her lips in, she wanted to argue his theory. She'd enjoy a life free of pain just fine. Of course, she wouldn't know it was free of pain if she'd never experienced it, just like she wouldn't appreciate companionship if she hadn't ever been without it. The man had a point. No way would she rejoice over the evil in her life, but she could see that she'd used it in a positive fashion. Poor Abby had turned it in on herself.

Martha's voice interrupted her thoughts. "May I see the last crystal?"

Nora slowly opened the cramped hand she'd clenched tightly through Martha's screams. The stone appeared tiny in her hand, but a few of the sharp edges bit into her skin. Droplets of blood decorated the yellow mineral. She moved to wipe the blood on her shirt.

Martha held up her hand to halt her. "Stop. It is as it should be. Leave the blood."

She placed the blood-stained stone in the woman's hand, expecting her to scream in pain. Instead, her fingers wrapped around it and held it for a few seconds. "Good news. Your sweetheart will come to you even as evil stalks you."

It would be wonderful if Clayton could come here. There was so much she wanted to show him. Maybe prove to Tonya that she wasn't just making him up. The specter of evil she could do without, though. "How can this happen when he is in another century?"

Martha allowed the stone to fall to the table. It rolled toward the silver one but veered away, almost seeming to be repelled. Even the stones recognized evil.

The woman sighed. "I can tell you only what I see. What I see is only one interpretation of events."

That didn't sound good. "You mean Clayton might not rescue me? I will be on my own against the big evil?"

The woman signaled to Owen. He stood and circled the table with a broom, sweeping up the salt in circular passes.

Martha placed her hands on the table, making sure not to touch the gray rock. "Well, I'd like to tell you that you won't be on your own, but I don't know."

"That sucks." Nora crossed her arms, not happy about leaving this place and going out to where something lurked.

Owen finished with the salt and took his seat quietly. "You can avoid danger. Anything that seems iffy, don't bother with it."

Despite the merits of Owen's plan, about sixty percent of what she did was iffy, from visiting the shop to riding the bus to working at the diner late at night with its unlocked back door. She didn't care if Barb did gripe when she found out about her locking the door. The door was staying locked. "Is this negative force close by?"

Martha pressed her hand over her heart. "It is very close. I can't say when, because the Fates don't work that way. If you listen, they will give you warning, and then you have to decide what to do with it."

Nora stood. This was the same type of cryptic talk her Nana always spouted. She needed hard facts: Stay home on Saturday between one and four to avoid a painful death.

In addition, why now, when it looked as though she could make something out of her life?

Even the thought of walking out the door and catching the bus made her knees shake. Resting her hands on the table, she tried to catch her balance. Didn't she come from a tough family? Hadn't her younger sister faced down her fears in both centuries? How could Nora do any less?

"Owen, we're driving this young lady home," Martha announced in a tone that also told them she did not expect any discussion on the matter.

The man jingled the car keys, anticipating the order.

"Wait, you don't want to take me home. It is a long way from here. Besides, it would cut into your business time." Nora secretly was glad of the offer, but did not want to take advantage of the couple. While there had been customers when she'd come before, no one lingered outside the doors waiting for it to reopen. "Stop fussing," Martha ordered. "We are taking you home. Besides, most of our business is online. Our real business is looking after humanity. What was your name?"

"Nora." She wondered why the woman who'd seemed to know all the hidden facets of her life hadn't already known.

Owen chuckled behind her. "Nora, granddaughter of Buell Hare. No way could we ever let you come to harm. Most people fear Esmeralda's wrath, but I know enough to keep from running afoul of Buell as well."

What was the man talking about? He'd gotten her grandparents' names right, though. "My grandparents are sweet, loving, elderly folks, not unlike you."

"Maybe so," Owen admitted with a grin. "You didn't know them when they were your age."

Martha pushed the back door open to a tiny parking lot that housed a worn-looking compact car. Nora briefly hoped the car could make it to her side of town.

Owen noticed her scrutiny of the car. "Don't worry about old Galahad there. He runs fine. I didn't know you were a Hare granddaughter until you got a determined look on your face that reminded me so much of Esmeralda. I thought I was the one time traveling. As far as I know, you have the only time-traveling family on the continent."

The man pushed the fob to release the door locks and hurried around to the passenger side to open the doors for Martha and her.

Safely ensconced in the car with her seat belt on, she gave her address to Owen.

Martha talked while Owen made his way out to the main street. "It makes sense why I would have such a strong reading with you. Your nana was always my dear friend. I suspect the amulet you're wearing was originally a gift from me to her. We are all tied together."

Nora considered her words. The Pagan community was often small and close-knit. It wasn't as unusual as it had first seemed that she might bump into someone who knew her grandparents.

The car slid through the neighborhood at a sedate pace, never stopping, even for stop signs. Obviously, the man didn't worry about the police. Through the tinted windows, she noticed two women dressed in crop tops, short skirts, and flamboyant blond wigs standing at the edge of the street, deep in conversation until the car came closer. Almost like windup toys, the two stopped talking and yanked up their tops as the car cruised by. Yep, the police had a little more to worry about here than someone slowly going through a stop sign.

It was like watching another world, one she wasn't a part of or familiar with. Two men in the shadows of the building exchanged money for something so small that the palm of the one man's hand covered it. The man quickly pocketed the money, spun away from his customer, and looked directly at Nora. She slumped in her seat, hoping he couldn't see her. A glance at his intense dark eyes warned her that the man could be very dangerous. If she'd walked to the bus, she might have passed him. Would she have witnessed the drug deal? Would he have felt obligated to kill her? Perhaps he was the evil lying in wait for her.

The car kept moving, gradually picking up speed as it moved out of the neighborhood, leaving the unknown menace behind. It would have been nice if the evil in Nora's life had been that stranger. She would be safe now. However, all future shop business would have to be the online sort.

Owen made a few rapid turns without warning as gunshots sounded behind them. Not a good neighborhood, that was for sure. It would have been easy for anyone to get in the way of a wayward bullet. Making herself as small as she could by sinking back in the upholstery, she noticed Martha did the same.

The buildings grew less ramshackle, still a little shabby but inhabitable, as they continued. There were planters of hardy geraniums and petunias on the stoops and children's abandoned toys on tiny patches of green. Small houses standing shoulder to shoulder gave away to small businesses, restaurants, and a tiny Mexican grocery. Young people strolled in groups, sometimes in pairs, and a few alone. Their shirts bore band names or goofy slogans identifying them as college students, as did their laughter and smiles. While this section of town might not be affluent, it did have a wealth of ambition and hope in the students who swelled the population to twice its normal size. Those same students kept pizza parlors, Laundromats, and liquor stores in the black. Nora briefly wondered what would happen to the city if the college pulled out. The thought was abandoned as soon as she conceived it.

The city could take care of itself. Her job was to locate evil and avoid it. Wasn't that every woman's natural instinct? Threats took different forms. Early on, she'd learned to pick up tacks, needles, and other sharp objects to save her feet. In school, she'd managed not to garner the attention of the mean girls by being too vocal or pretty. On the street, she knew not to make eye contact with the disgusting men whose eyes devoured her as if they owned her body. Knowing all that, she never truly escaped the tendrils of malevolence.

Martha half-turned to look at her. "I hope you don't have to go anywhere today. We can do a protection spell as we leave."

The thought initially comforted her as she thought of watching movies and eating whatever healthy concoction Tonya whipped up. Then she remembered work. No way, she could not go in. No need to mention it to the old couple after all they'd done. It would only make them worry. She'd managed to take care of herself for years. No reason to believe anything would happen today. She crossed her fingers, realizing it would do no good, but hey, it couldn't hurt.

CHAPTER TWELVE

Martha and Owen insisted on walking her upstairs to her apartment. They would not leave until they saw her safely locked inside. She swung the door open only to realize the apartment was empty. Similar to rooms seen in furniture stores, the apartment had the appearance of a home but without any texture. The lack of sound was her first indication. A human in residence created a disturbance in the air. As a fellow human, she found this disturbance usually preferable, especially now. She needed someone to talk to about her latest issue.

Smiling at the older couple, she gestured to the living room. "Home, sweet home."

Martha took a slow appraisal of the room. "Where's your roommate?"

The question startled her, because she was sure she'd never mentioned Tonya. "Um, I don't know. I expected her to be here since she wasn't feeling well." It would have been a disservice to mention her friend was hung-over. Tonya seldom overindulged. Ogden would drive a Baptist to drink.

Owen began to prowl through the small apartment, opening closets, which was a big mistake. He swung open the hall closet only to have skis and ski poles assault him, remnants of her roommate's flirtation with cross-country skiing that hadn't lasted more than a week. Nora rushed forward to disentangle the man from the sporting equipment.

"What are you looking for?" Exasperation colored her voice.

"Prowler." Owen uprighted a ski and pushed it back into the closet.

It probably wouldn't be a good time to point out that an elderly man didn't stand a chance if the prowler had a gun.

The man managed a slight grin. "I know, you're thinking what help could an old man be. I know a few things that could stop a man in his tracks, as does Martha. Then there's you, too. Three is always better than one."

Nora bent to gather up the ski boots and waterproof gloves that had tumbled to the floor. Rising, she nodded to Owen. "Good point. Feel free to look in the other rooms, but be warned, most of the closets are a bit stuffed."

Martha examined objects in the living room, picking them up and putting them down. Seeing Nora, she lifted her eyebrows. "Good news."

"Oh." Maybe the woman would tell her they'd somehow bypassed the threat. A few steps brought her closer to Martha, who was examining a glass whale Nora had purchased at a yard sale.

She placed the whale back on the shelf. Throwing out both arms, Martha slowly turned. "Lots of good energy. I see two young women living clean, promoting positive energy, and honoring the Gods and Goddesses. No imprint of evil here."

Inhaling deeply, Nora waited. She could pretty much bet there would be a "but" tacked on to the thought. The woman looked thoughtful and pointed to a spot on the couch.

"Recently, there has been someone in your apartment. I think he or she sat there. There's deadness about this individual. No love, no vitality." She cocked her head, twisted her lips slightly. "I would almost say soulless, but he or she is more of an individual who has never really learned how to live."

"Ogden. You described him perfectly. You didn't sense any evil about him?" She'd wondered earlier, if he'd been the menace, but rejected the idea as soon as it occurred. Placing two fingers on her temple, Martha looked at the couch. "This Ogden is basically selfish. He does not mean you intentional harm, but..."

That was a relief. Her gaze danced over everything in the room, trying to see the décor as a stranger would. Tonya insisted on tacking up a four-foot-square poster that portrayed hoodoo symbols in concentric circles. She often wondered why she never had any dates after they'd been in the apartment. Most of her dates were probably worried about her collecting hair strands and nail parings to make a doll in their image. Failure to bring flowers might result in a sharp pin jabbed through the doll.

Nora knew Tonya wasn't like that, but non-pagan folks held close stereotypes they'd collected in darkened movie theatres as the true way of things.

Their secondhand furniture sported bold geometric-print cushions that Tonya had stitched up. An old battered flat-topped trunk served as their coffee table. A handful of live plants added greenery and vitality to the small room. There were only a few items that were hers. The brass candelabra Nana claimed belonged to Nora's great-grandmother and a small brass wolf figurine. Martha drifted over to the candelabra and stroked it lightly.

"Much history here. Your entire family tree is impressed into this one object. Esme left a definite imprint." She chuckled to herself. "Your grandmother was a wild woman. All the women wanted to be her, but all the men just wanted her, even if they were afraid of her."

It was an uncomfortable way of thinking of her nana, but Nora could still see traces of the same woman in her feisty, opinionated manner. What was it she'd wanted to ask Martha? Oh, she remembered. "Um, you say Ogden was basically harmless, but you hesitated and never finished your sentence."

Martha's hand fell from the candelabra she was examining. "Yes, this I did, because I did not want to alarm you anymore than needed."

Great. Nora blew out her breath. It was going to be like pulling off a bandage. "Tell me. Knowledge is power. Don't you watch the commercials?"

Owen walked into the room, stood behind Martha, and placed his hands on her slender shoulders. "Tell her," he urged.

"The man himself is shallow, a tool," Martha began.

The description surprised a laugh out of Nora. Many people called Ogden a tool. Others had much worse names for him.

The woman ignored the laugh and continued. "It will be easy for those with a stronger will to manipulate him and use him against you. Be on your guard."

Well, that didn't seem to be too scary. Her plan was to continue to avoid Ogden. Maybe that meant she'd inadvertently miss any evil directed her way. "I can do that."

Martha pulled a bottle out of her handbag. "Good. Before we go, I want to anoint your windows and doors."

She and Tonya had already done that, but a little extra help was always welcome. She followed the couple room to room while they touched the windowsills with their fingers, murmuring a protection prayer at each opening. After bidding them good-bye and closing the door, Nora could hear them murmuring prayers on the other side. To think she'd wondered why her neighbors kept a wide berth of her and Tonya.

The sound of her visitors' footsteps on the stairs as they left reinforced her aloneness. Nora twisted on the portable radio they kept in the kitchen. She had to adjust the dial a millimeter at a time as if searching for signals from other planets to find her favorite station. Her reward for her effort was a tinny sound often interrupted by static. She had paid only a dollar for it at the local thrift store. It was probably older than she was. The high-pitched whine it made as it failed to grab the station signal grated on her already frayed nerves.

Clicking off the radio, she picked up the remote and aimed it at their flat-screen television. It was the only actual theft-worthy item in their abode. Tonya had won it in a bingo game down the street. She'd had to ask for help to move it and had paraded down the street with her cargo and helpers. Since the box identified it as a television, they'd expected it to disappear within days. Ironically, it hadn't. Maybe the rumors portraying the two of them as a witchy pair had paid off.

The first image on the television screen was a frightened woman pressing an alarm while a burglar ransacked her home. It was only commercial, but Nora didn't need to see that. A barrage of gunfire came with the channel change to a Western. Normally, she liked Westerns. The idea of people carving out new lives for themselves on the frontier appealed to her. However, what Hollywood depicted as real had very little to do with what had actually happened.

She changed the channel again. This time to an infomercial with scantily clad women who insisted the featured product had improved their love lives. This particular infomercial usually came on later at night. She glanced at the time in the corner of the television. It was 12:58.

Her shift started at two. She'd have to catch the 1:15 bus. She needed to change into her cook whites. Forget about eating anything. She could get food at the diner.

She poked at her stomach to judge whether it was getting any softer after her numerous meals there. Maybe. Put that on the list of things she didn't need to think about.

Grabbing her clothes, she headed to the bathroom. Why did she have to go to work, when Doug seemed to take off whenever he felt like it? For Pete's sake, it had been her day off. Splashing water on her face, she continued her mental rant. Anger felt better than fear.

Her hairbrush kept snagging on a snarl at the back of her neck. Twisting the necklace around caused a sharp yank on the back of her scalp. Great, her hair was tangled up in the chain. That's what she got for not trimming her hair. A quick snip would free the charm. Her hands were on the haircutting scissors she kept in the bathroom, but she hesitated. Didn't she want to grow her hair out as a symbolic gesture that her past no longer dictated her choices? The rape had been the reason she'd cut off her hair. Putting down the scissors, she decided to work the chain free. Unclasping it, she tugged the smaller clasp end through her hair.

Gently pulling the tendrils from the other half of the chain, she managed to free the necklace without sacrificing any hair. A quick glance at her watch had her swearing under her breath. That operation had taken longer than it should have. Pulling on her white top, she decided to forgo brushing her teeth. As it was, she'd have to run to the bus stop. Grabbing the small backpack that often served as a purse, she headed out the door.

Taking the steps two at a time, she made the landing in faster than usual. The bus was on time for a change. The vehicle's throaty roar and gagging diesel fumes gave her the extra burst of speed. The lumbering bus shuddered to a stop in front of the Plexiglas bus shelter. Several people crowded around the bus entrance, working their way onto the bus as Nora broke into a full-out run.

Two teen boys cheered her on, or more appropriately jeered her on. "Run, Forrest, run."

No time to glare at them. Her only mode of transportation was getting ready to depart. Someone on the bus pointed to her. The bus driver reopened the doors he had closed.

"Just made it, Little Missy," he commented as she staggered onto the bus.

Normally, she'd tell him her name wasn't Little Missy. Instead, she flashed her bus pass and collapsed into the nearest seat. That unexpected run had emphasized her need to work out on a more consistent basis and eat less burgers, starting tomorrow. The familiar scenery flew by as she bemoaned the fact she'd missed Tonya. Digging through her backpack, she located her phone to text her friend.

Got weird news at the shop. Will tell u later. Let no strangers into the apartment, not even Ogden.

Her hair was probably a mess after her impromptu dash. Running her fingers through, she tried to comb it into some semblance of a hairstyle as opposed to her impersonation of a homeless person. Her fingers slid down the back of her neck, feeling the lengthening strands. Something was wrong. Her thumb rubbed across her neck. It was bare. Her right hand slapped against her upper chest, searching for the amulet. Where was it?

An image of her necklace on the bathroom sink came to mind. She'd left it in her rush to catch the bus. Her fingers lingered at her neck wanting the reassurance it provided. She could text Tonya, but it wasn't exactly like someone would break into their apartment and steal it. It would be there when she got home. She tried to calm herself. Come nine o' clock, she'd be home.

The diner came into view. She stood up, eager to get her shift over with. The bus door had barely opened when she shot out of it like a sprinter from the starter block, gasping by the time she reached the door of the diner and swung it open. Bonnie gave her a disgusted look as she leaned against the inside wall. Moving closer, the waitress leaned across the counter to address Nora privately, meaning only half of the patrons could hear her.

"You're getting as bad as alien-phobic Barney. You'll have to start wearing a ball cap lined with aluminum foil. Were the giant mosquitoes going to grab you and carry you away?"

Two nearby men, hunkered over pie and coffee, laughed at Bonnie's comments. Nora worked on slowing her breathing and settled for fixing the server with a stare that promised retribution. No way could she explain what was going on. It didn't make sense even to her.

A quick visual inspection showed a handful of usual customers and a family dressed in matching shirts, which identified them as tourists. They must have been going to the nearby theme park. A few looked up at her entrance, but most looked away, except for Bonnie, who raised an eyebrow. Refusing to answer her inquiry, Nora headed toward the kitchen.

The smell of onions and the jump in temperature hit her as she pushed open the door. OSHA had come through once and required a fan for the cook's comfort. Barb had mounted the fan with strict instructions not to turn it on. The fan tended to cool the food and made too much noise for the cook to actually hear the orders. Various cooks would plug the fan in just to cool off for a few seconds between rushes. Ernie had the fan going and didn't hear her enter. He jumped about a foot when she reached for a paper cook hat.

"Whoa! Don't sneak up on me like that!"

Nora made a mental note not to use the fan. She couldn't take a chance on not being aware. "Hey, I'm sorry. The fan makes such a racket you didn't hear me." She had to yell the words to be heard over the fan and the sizzling meat.

Ernie pulled the plug with one hand. "Hey, what are you doing here? Isn't it your day off? As a young single gal, aren't you supposed to be out enjoying yourself?"

"I wish." Nora felt that the media image of college students engaging in numerous hookups did her no favors. Knotting her oversized apron in the front, she added, "Doug called in."

Ernie snorted. "Yeah, that's right. Barb did say something to me earlier. I guess it went in one ear and out the other. Thing is, he's off more than he works. Well, I hope he decides to come to work when it's my day off. The missus is not a fan of me working seven days a week."

Nora wasn't fond of working seven days a week, either. Her joints ached from lack of sleep. Had it been only last night that she was helping Clayton with an epidemic? It felt like forever ago. Lack of sleep was making her irritable on top of already being paranoid.

The fry beeper went off, sending her into action. Pulling the wire basket out of the hot oil, she hooked it on to the bar and bounced it twice to shake off the residual grease before dumping it into the fry station. Ernie had five plates set out, which meant she needed to get five servings out of the fries. Ernie was good at his job, so she had no doubt there would be enough potatoes to go around. Too bad Ernie wasn't the relief cook. If he were, then she'd be at home enjoying her day off. She'd probably be sleeping right now. The thought of a nap tempted her. Who knew that at the grand age of twenty-three she'd be yearning for a snooze rather like a senior citizen?

Ernie hummed under his breath as he placed burgers onto the open buns. Scooping up the fries, she deposited a stack on each plate. She watched as he capped the burgers. Picking up the plates, three on her first trip and two on her second, she delivered them to the window. Seeing that Bonnie's back was turned, she pummeled the bell with relish, startling the waitress and drawing attention as she announced, "Order up."

Yeah, it was petty of her. Stupid, too, since she'd have to spend the next six hours with an irate co-worker.

Bonnie mainly flirted with the customers, but the woman majored in spiteful. Good thing Nora was the cook. She hated to imagine the vindictive things the woman might do to the food if their situations had been reversed. Yep, she could expect a night of window silence. No bells, no calls, she'd have to keep checking for order slips to keep Bonnie from lambasting her for being slow on the food.

Nora watched Ernie leave with a wave, letting the back door slam behind him. Nora stared at the door for a few seconds, wishing she'd been the one who'd left. She darted toward it, securing the lock. A quick glance over her shoulder assured her there was no Barb on the premises. Sometimes the manager was up in her office, behind the two-way mirror counting money or watching the employees. Today would have been a day she made certain to slip out early to avoid listening to both her and Brandon griping about working extra hours for the missing Doug.

Brandon. Good Goddess, she had to deal with him, too. Well, she could pretend nothing had happened, which might have been the case. The man had been very friendly the last time they'd worked together. She did not look forward to trying to explain to him the weirdness that constituted her life.

Gathering the prep pans, she stacked them in the dishwasher tray. She'd have a couple of hours to think of some reasonable explanation for Tonya's claim that she was hooking up with him.

A knock on the door reminded her that she'd locked the back door. Red-faced, she opened it for the bread guy, while pretending surprise. "Was the door locked? Goodness, I wonder if Ernie tripped the lock when he went out." She crossed her fingers, hoping Ernie would forgive her for throwing him under the bus.

The bread man grunted and backed into the narrow kitchen with his tall load of bun trays. He moved the new rack near the fridge, and then pulled out a couple trays of buns from the old rack before   he pushed it out the door with him. The man never said anything, didn't even look at her. Nora made sure to lock the door again. Not everyone was a talker, but he was plain creepy. Thinking about the man made her shiver. He wasn't the usual delivery guy, which meant he couldn't be the evil she needed to avoid. It had to be someone she met on a regular basis.

Something made her turn quickly and look at the window. A scrap of paper fluttered in the breeze created by the closing door. How long had that been there? So began Bonnie's revenge. Snatching the paper, she found it was for a fish sandwich platter. Didn't get that too much. Opening the freezer, she grabbed the box of fish fillets and carried them to the stainless steel counter. She made a mental note to replace the box as she dropped the fry basket into the oil. The walleye would taste a little bit like fries, but so far, no one had complained.

Bonnie's voice, reminiscent of nails on a chalkboard, carried through the window. "Did you break out the fishing pole to go catch me a walleye platter?"

The order could not have been there for more than a minute, and she knew it. Nora decided to be the better person and say nothing. Well, she wasn't exactly being the better person. She just didn't have anything pithy to say. She could hear Bonnie slinging dishes around in the front and hoped the diners enjoyed the show.

Most of her shift went the same way. Her eyes stayed trained on the window, ready for the appearance of the elusive scrap of paper for her to pounce on. In the end, she rang the bell every time she delivered an order. There was no reason for a customer to suffer due to the help's bad attitude. A quick glance at the clock reminded her when her shift was minutes away from ending. Bonnie's attitude kept her mind off the back door and things that went bump in the night. In less than an hour, she'd be home with her feet up on the trunk, telling Tonya about everything that had happened today, including Bonnie's six-hour-long hissy fit.

A metallic jingle announced another customer. Bonnie greeted him with a hearty, "Hello, handsome."

That's how she greeted all the men who showed up without female company, which made her a popular server.

A familiar masculine voice answered her. "Hello, yourself."

Brandon was here. It was his agreed-upon time to help cover Doug's shift, but Nora wasn't ready. Too busy anticipating Bonnie's sneak orders, she'd never developed a story to explain everything in a way that would almost sound normal. The bell jingled again.

"I wasn't done talking to you, soldier boy," a belligerent voice called out.

A drunk? As if, she needed that, too. Let Brandon handle him. He was the only one with muscle to boot the guy out. Maybe she should call the police. Her hand hovered over the black wall phone, ready to press nine, when the man spoke again.

"I'm not giving up Nora. Had a good thing going with—" The voice choked off.

Ogden? Damn, she was going to have to deal with this side of him. He had to be drunk. Why else would he act like this? Nothing was on the grill, so she was free to go out there and attempt to make her personal life a little less public.

Not sure what she would say, she hit the swinging door at half-jog, only to find Brandon with a chokehold on Ogden's Oxford shirt. Despite Ogden's height, Brandon still managed to get the man up on his tiptoes. Ogden's eyes bulged as he gasped something about suing everyone.

Brandon growled his reply. "I don't care if you're a medical doctor. I'll tell you what you aren't—smart. Nora's done with you. She wants someone without ice water in his veins." He shook Ogden for emphasis before letting go of his shirt.

Ogden smoothed the creases, muttering something about lawsuits. Several of the patrons were quick to volunteer to serve as witnesses that Brandon was the one who was assaulted first.

Ogden backed toward the door. He cast an angry look at Nora.

Nora knew it was time to make the break clean. "We're through, Ogden. I found my soul mate. You better hurry. The police are on their way."

Ogden darted out the diner door to the delight of the patrons. A few called out physically impossible suggestions.

Brandon pivoted, taking Nora's hand. "I wouldn't call us soul mates, but I wouldn't mind researching the subject with you." He gave her his most charming smile, causing one of the female customers to "aw" in response.

She snatched back her hand. Could anything else go wrong tonight? "I didn't mean you."

One man yelped, "Ooh, that stung. Damned if you do, damned if you don't." His three companions laughed at his remark.

Nora had had enough. She was going home and none too soon. She headed for the kitchen but threw over her shoulder, "Clayton's my soul mate."

"Who's Clayton?" Brandon asked.

She pushed open the kitchen door to grab her stuff. Brandon was on his own as far as cleaning. A brief survey revealed there really wasn't that much to clean, anyhow. The loud rumble of the fan drew her attention upward. She hadn't turned it on. If no one had been back there, then how did it get on? A hand with odd-smelling cloth muffled her mouth before she could even consider screaming. A needle plunged into her arm. Things grew blurry. The evil had found her.

Chapter Thirteen

A dripping sound was off to her right. Nora kept her eyes tightly shut, buying herself time. A musty smell permeated the air, along with the smell of sauerkraut. Was she in the basement of a German restaurant? Kidnapped to cook sauerbraten against her will? She knew better. The whimsical musing helped her to not freak out.

Rolling on the lumpy mattress, she tested her muscles. Rope tied both her ankles and wrists. It felt like regular rope, not that what kind it was mattered too much. The important thing was she couldn't use her limbs. What if he were sitting there watching her? The thought creeped her out. Opening her senses as her grandfather had taught her, she swept the room. No human, but there seemed to be rodents. Ick. Not rats. She didn't think she could bear the thought of rats chewing on her fingers. True, she realized she was supposed to honor all life-forms. Honoring worked much better when she didn't meet some of the creatures up close and personal.

Slowly, she opened her eyes to a dim textile weave. Blindfolded. Damn, was there anything he hadn't done?

A sense of light penetrated the fabric. He must have left a light on. Why?

She had to be smart, calm, and logical. Apparently, she'd screwed up, even when there had been so many warnings on different levels. Foolishly, she'd overcome her instinctual reaction by rationalizing why the warnings hadn't merited serious consideration. Early on, she'd felt evil roll off the man. Instead of doing everything she could to avoid him, she'd simply counted him as one of the diner's offbeat regulars.

People have instincts for a reason her mother was fond of pointing out. Locking the diner's back door had done little good when she'd been taken through it. He had to have been inside. Hiding in the bathroom?

Now it was time to use the intelligence she prided herself for. An unconscious person, especially a blindfolded one, wouldn't need a light. The light might be for him or a camera.

Right now, he could be in another room, watching her on a monitor. Her reprieve would last as long as he thought she was out. Stilling her movements, she tried to act as if she were still under the drug's influence. Luckily, at the hospital she'd witnessed enough people under anesthesia, who could not even blink, let alone move, to mimic them.

Holding herself rigid, she took inventory of her body. Clothes were all on. Thank the Goddess. Her shoes were missing. Some chafing on her wrists and ankles from the rope appeared to be the extent of her injuries. Her stomach growled, letting her know its empty state. She couldn't remember when she'd last eaten. Her bladder urged her to get up and relieve its fullness. Not that she needed one more thing to worry about.

If only she had help. Did anyone know she was gone? Brandon and Bonnie might have assumed she'd left in a huff, slamming out the back door instead of the front to avoid them. Nora bit her lip. She'd have thought the same unless there was a tip-off. Was her backpack still there? Had whoever taken her known enough to pick it up? Did Tonya miss her yet?

She had told her they would talk when Nora returned home. She and her roommate were the opposite of social butterflies. They spent most of their evenings together at home, similar to an old married couple. Surely, Tonya would be worried by now. Still, what could she do?

If Tonya called the diner, Brandon might say Nora had left in a huff. The police would say she was over twenty-one and could do what she wanted. Her roommate might hint at foul play. The police would take her report but consider her being missing the result of too much partying and assume that she was sleeping it off somewhere. No doubt, Tonya would call her family, who would hop into the car and immediately drive up. If anyone could whip the police into action, Nana could. Still, how would they know where to look?

There was nothing to identify her location. She might not even still be in the city. If she'd had her backpack, her phone would be in it. The police could use the GPS unit in it to track her. A small spark of hope flared. Then the memory of a television show in which the kidnapper had taped the woman's cell phone to her dog's collar and left it alongside the road stomped out the spark. Whoever had her could have searched her bag and dropped her phone far from her actual location.

If only, there was some way to reach her family. At one time, her grandfather, or even her sister Leah, had read people's minds on close contact. Maybe they could help her. All she needed to do was get a message to them. Squeezing her eyes shut, she concentrated on her grandfather's face. Nothing.

Nora, where are you? What is happening?

Clayton's voice calmed her a little. Maybe he could help. But how, being stuck in another century? As far as she knew, he could talk to her only because of their soul mate bond.

Clayton, I need help. Someone has kidnapped me. I don't know why. I was warned evil was looking for me. I am tied up and blindfolded.

Oh, my sweet darling, I will kill the monster that would do such a thing.

He growled the last few words, demonstrating his anger. Unfortunately, there was no way Clayton could touch the malicious creature.

How did I come to you? The few times I crossed over into your time I don't remember doing anything special. Maybe I could cross over now.

The thought excited her. She'd had the way to escape all along.

Hurry now, sweetheart, come to me. Clayton's voice conveyed urgency.

Squeezing her eyes shut, she concentrated on his handsome face, willing herself to be beside her soul mate.

I am coming, Clayton.

Her voice sounded loud. She must have said the words aloud. Now, Mr. Creepy might come investigate. Everything felt the same, though. She was still horizontal on an uncomfortable cot mattress in a damp basement as opposed to being in the past with her sweetheart.

Clayton, it didn't work. Why didn't it work?

The urge to cry tempted her. It wouldn't help anything.

What had been different before? She had always been asleep when she'd slipped back into the past. She thought of Clayton often during the day, but did not pop out of her time. What was the difference?

Time travel was theoretically impossible. Grandpa Buell had slipped through a time portal, which many people readily concurred, could exist. Leah had commented that she'd felt pulled back in time by a previous life. Maybe that was why she could go back, but Nora's previous lives were associated with Clayton.

His voice returned as if hearing his name. *I've given it some thought. The times you came to me, I needed you sorely. Perhaps my need was so intense you felt it.*

The thought had some merit. She heard the sound of a door rattling to her right, followed by a feminine voice. "Hello, hello? Is there somebody there? I'm Ellie. I am locked up in this room. I don't know how long I've been here."

Nora held herself perfectly still. Was this a test? Was she being filmed? Her mind rushed through the probabilities of someone else being the victim of the kidnapper. "Ellie, I'm Nora." Her voice was low and raspy, reflecting her dry throat.

"I'm here," a surprisingly young voice answered. "I heard him bring you down last night. He ordered me not to talk to you, but he's gone now. I heard the door slam when he left. I think he actually has a job when he's not kidnapping women. You're the cook he talked about grabbing."

He'd talked about grabbing her. No wonder she'd had premonitions. "Are we—does he have a camera set up monitoring us?" Nora could picture a small camera mounted in the corner of the room. Ellie could be wrong. The man could thunder down the steps at any moment, realizing she'd awakened.

The woman made a derisive noise. "No, I doubt the man would be smart enough to operate one. Then again, he was sneaky enough to pick me off the street. I never saw a camera, though."

Picked her off the street? She sounded so young.

Ellie spoke, her voice resigned and weary. "I was holding up a sign to sell fireworks along 38, a real busy road. I thought the female owner was the creep because she kept insisting I wear a bikini top and short-shorts. My mom was totally against it. I wouldn't do it until Kayla, my boss, offered me an extra twenty. My mom was already at work, so I figured I'd get back and change before she knew."

"Fireworks," Nora said, thinking aloud. "It must have been before the Fourth of July."

"Yes, that's right," Ellie agreed. "What month is it now?"

She didn't want to tell the young girl that months of her life had trickled away while she'd remained trapped in this dungeon. "Ellie, how old are you?"

"Sixteen. No, wait. I had a birthday while I've been locked up. I am seventeen now and missing my senior year at school." The girl's sigh carried more information than her words.

A sixteen-year-old girl being picked up by some perv wasn't right. Her only perceived crime was being female.

Clayton's voice nudged her away from imagining the various violations committed against women. *I think if I concentrate hard enough I can come to you.*

That would be wonderful. Not only could he rescue her, but they could free Ellie, too. *Please try. There's another woman here who needs your help, too.*

Time and the laws of a normal universe will not keep me from your side. The sound of his familiar lilt reassured her.

Then he was gone. She felt his absence. Where would he go to find the help he needed?

Ellie asked her something.

"What did you say?"

"I asked where you were when he grabbed you."

Nora tried to work herself into a sitting position. Lying prone on the mattress made her feel too much like a sacrifice. She managed to wiggle her feet over the edge while trying to swing her body into an upright position. Her bare feet slapped the floor, sending a tremor up her legs and reminding her of her urgent need to pee. Sitting up made her feel a little better. She imagined she looked like one of those stone pharaoh statues with her tied hands and feet keeping her in a rigid posture. "He grabbed me at work. I am so mad at myself for letting it happen."

"I know what you mean." Ellie snorted. It was hard to tell if it was a cough or a sign of disgust. "My mom kept telling me I was sheltered because I went to Catholic school. I thought I had street cred. What a joke. He pulled up in white panel van. Ya know, the one the crime shows always have the killers using. That should have been a hint. He wanted me to look at some fireworks he'd bought that didn't work right. I told him it wasn't my job. He should go into the store to complain. He kept asking me just to look at them. I thought if I humored him, he'd go away. No sooner than I peered into the van, he pushed me and stuck a needle in my side. Something hit my head, too. I may have screamed. I can't remember. I just remember waking up here, like you."

"Oh." Nora didn't know what else to say. It didn't look good, considering Ellie had been there awhile. Since Ellie was a minor, the police had probably pulled out all the stops to search for her. Her mother had probably gone public, making tearful pleas on television. "Wait a minute. I think I saw an Amber Alert for you on television. I remember a photo of a blond girl standing by a horse."

"That's my Kimber. I compete with her in junior steeplechase. Well, I did. At least Mom used a good photo and not my horrible school picture. I never even got my senior pictures taken. I had an appointment the week after. Had it all planned out. The photographer was coming to my dad's place so Kimber could be in the photos." Ellie's words choked off as she began to weep.

"Ellie, Ellie, listen there are two of us now, two smart women against one male criminal. Surely, we can make that work in our favor. Tell me about the first day. What happened?" If Nora knew what to prepare herself for, she'd be ready.

The crying tapered off. Ellie inhaled deeply, loudly gulped before starting. "I don't know how long I was out. I remember waking up tied up and wearing an adult diaper. You've probably got one on, too."

Nora shifted on the cot, hearing a telltale crinkle and feeling bulkiness in her pants. Ooh, she didn't even want to think about him putting it on her. "Yes, go on."

"I think he does that because he's gone more than he's here. I'm not even sure if this is his regular home. He might go home to a wife and kids, which somehow makes it worse."

Ellie was getting off track. "Tell me about the first day," Nora urged.

"By the time I saw him, I was starving, thirsty, and had to go to the bathroom. I refused to use the diaper, but I wish I had now."

"Why?" Nora knew she wouldn't like the answer.

Ellie cleared her throat. "He walked me to the bathroom with my hands still tied. He pulled my shorts down, watched me pee, and then raped me. In the tiny bathroom, where there was no place to escape, and my hands were tied."

Nora could hear the self-blame in her voice. "Ellie, stop blaming yourself."

"Maybe if I hadn't listened to my boss and worn the bikini top, I'd be at St. Ignatius instead of here." The clatter of things falling and a few hard kicks at the door echoed off concrete walls.

"Stop thinking like that. They want you to believe that so they don't have to be accountable for their actions. I see guys all the time running with their shirts off. Good-looking, fit men, but they don't have women throwing them into panel vans. As women, we blame ourselves for men violating us. Trust me. I know." She blew out a breath after her long speech.

Ellie voice sounded hesitant. "Has this happened to you before? That must really suck."

Nora thought back to Owen's words about how bad things can change the course of your life. It certainly had hers. Now, it was time to use that information to help someone else. "I wasn't kidnapped. My friend Abby and I were leaving school late at night. We'd been working on the school newspaper. We drove together. It was winter, which meant early nightfall."

If her hands hadn't been bound, she probably would have dropped her head into them. She'd never told anyone, except for Clayton, and she never really told him, either. He'd just picked it up while tiptoeing through her mind. Nora shifted on the cot suddenly feeling as if someone sat down beside her. "Abby and I were talking. I remember being happy, laughing. Abby was telling me about this guy she liked flirting with her. Then, suddenly all these football players surrounded us. They were still wearing their practice jerseys. At first, I had no clue what they wanted. One of them grinned and said, 'I hear witchy sex is really hot.'"

"What did he mean? I know I am sheltered, but I've never heard of witchy sex."

Nora cleared her throat again. "Abby and I are both witches. The other students knew it. For the most part, they were cool with it, or so I thought. I'm not sure what the football players' reasoning was, but we were there for the taking, or so they thought."

"As a witch, couldn't you cast a spell and freeze them in place?" There was a curious lift in her voice.

"Common misconception. Being a witch sometimes involves spells or incantations, but it is more about the person finding her path as opposed to people flying through the air. It isn't like in the movies. If I dislike someone, a huge wind doesn't blow him away. If that were the case, then no witches would have burned at the stake. My confidence in my various protective amulets led me to act in an unsafe manner, though."

"What could you have done? You were at school. You were supposed to be safe there."

That's what she'd thought, too. She'd thought being a witch was enough to keep her safe, despite all the harm witches had suffered in the past at the hands of misguided individuals. "Neither one of us was paying attention to our surroundings. We had a guard at school. We could have asked him to walk out with us. I had my keys in my purse. I could have had them wrapped around my fingers to use as a weapon. Looking back, I see there was a lot we could have done."

"How many were there?"

Nora pondered the question for a minute. They'd seemed to be everywhere. Grabbing her, holding Abby, and dragging them to the darkest part of the lot where a trio of tall pines had thrown shadows, blocking out the security lights. "I don't know. I remember one held a hand over my mouth and my wrists tight. There was one at each leg holding me down and another one raping me. That would be four on me alone. I am not sure about Abby. Did someone hold her and force her to watch or were there more? I only remember now that they switched off without ever releasing my arms or legs, as if they had done it before." Nora bit down hard on her bottom lip. They had done it before. Of course, they had. They'd kept on doing it.

"That's horrible. Did you call the police?" Ellie's tone carried the unspoken message that, of course, a woman would call the police.

In retrospect, Nora's decision not to call the police seemed cowardly. "No, when they were done, they threatened us. Told us they'd tell everyone we enticed them. Apparently, they'd been planning it. They'd already told several people we'd been coming on to them. What chance did we have against popular players? Two lone witches, you already know some of the stereotypes. I helped Abby to the car and drove her home. She asked me to tell no one. Her parents were out for an anniversary dinner. I put her in the shower, where she just stood there not talking or moving. I stepped into the shower with my clothes on, scrubbed her and shampooed her hair. I tried to scour away every mark those monsters put on her. I dressed her and put her to bed. I took her clothes with me and threw them in a neighbor's trashcan. That was the last time Abby ever spoke about the incident."

"Oh," Ellie said softly. "You never saw your friend again?"

"I saw her several times in the facility her parents placed her in, but she never talked again. I know she blamed herself, as I blamed myself. Something snapped in Abby. I'm not sure it can ever be fixed. I tried to explain what happened to her parents. At first, they were anxious to file a report. Her father was vocal about filing charges until I mentioned the names of the boys I recognized. One's father was a powerful trial attorney."

Nora coughed trying to clear her throat. "I remember his face when I said the name. He whispered something like, 'Not him, everyone would think he was trying to stir things up again.'"

"What did he mean?" Ellie's sounded as tired as Nora felt.

"At the time, I thought it was peculiar, especially after he was ready to call the police. Then I remembered Abby telling me her father had spent time in prison for embezzlement. Apparently the football player's father was the guy who put him there."

"Was he guilty?"

Odd, but she never considered the question too deeply. Abby hadn't thought he was and that was good enough for her. "I don't know. Maybe not, if he was so afraid of the lawyer. Their sudden desire to hush things up convinced me no good would come of filing a report."

Ellie sighed audibly. "Then you never said anything to your family."

"Never told my family, but being who they were they probably knew. Claimed to be sick for the rest of the week to avoid going to school. The next week we moved." It still amazed her that somehow her family had known. They'd said nothing. Even Leah and Ethan hadn't complained about the sudden move or the need for it.

"How could it be either one of your faults? Those animals planned it. Not much you could have done against all those muscular guys." Ellie gave the door a hard kick and yelped. "Mr. Creepy doesn't let you wear shoes. Too much of a chance of running."

"That was my point for you, Ellie. It didn't matter if you wore a bikini top or not. Abby and I had coats on. That didn't slow the guys down. This creep planned it. Why else would he be driving around with a syringe full of tranquilizer? If it hadn't been you, he might have found another girl by herself." Using her bound hands, Nora managed to raise them to scratch at her face, knocking off her blindfold in the process.

A couple of blinks helped her eyes adjust to the yellow pool of light a fluorescent bulb threw out. Definitely a basement. It looked more like a cellar with its dirt floor. There were stacks of some wood frames with bricks on them against one wall. Rocking on the cot, she tried to stand. Her first attempt ended with her face planted in the dirt. "Oomph."

"What are you doing?

Kneeling, Nora leaned against the cot, trying to get her butt back on it. "Trying to stand." Seated back on the cot, she scooted down the folding bed. The hopping hadn't worked too well. If she could get next to the wall, it might catch her. Turning, she made sure her shoulder touched the wall.

"Ouch, that hurt." Her legs proved to be a little shaky, maybe the result of the drug or lack of circulation. "Ellie, do you know what type of drug he used on you?"

Nora took one small hop that reminded her of her need to pee. Hopping was not advisable. Penguin walk it would be. Rocking side to side, she slowly made her way around the room. Who would have known that what she'd learned at summer camp would actually have some benefit?

Spider webs clung to the corners, while dust particles danced in the yellow light. Cleaning was not the man's strong point. Walking like Penguin from the old Batman movie, she made her way closer to the frames. A strong whiff of fermenting cabbage demonstrated her mind wasn't playing jokes on her. It really was sauerkraut. The trays of sauerkraut were stacked in front of a plywood wall. Hobbling closer, she almost jumped when Ellie's voice sounded closer.

"I'm not sure what he used. He joked about it being an animal tranquilizer and that he used too much on me."

Nora was close to the wall. Lifting her secured hands, she tapped on the plywood. "Are you in there?"

"Yes. You're up and around. I cried and prayed for days that someone would rescue me. No one did."

Working her way to the door, Nora leaned against it to be closer to the girl. "Don't give up hope. We'll get out of here. I think he used ketamine on us. It's called Special K. Possibly Telazol. Still, we both went out fast. Real fast."

She could feel Ellie's presence on the other side of the door, sensing it more than physically feeling. Her essence grew cooler as if the life were ebbing out of her.

"I want to believe, Nora, but I've been here so long. I watched him build the cage I'm in now. Even then, he was planning on taking you. In a couple of months, you'll watch him build another one. The fact I've seen his face means I'm never leaving. I think there is another girl upstairs, but I'm not sure. I thought I heard steps once, even singing."

A glance back at her abandoned blindfold chilled Nora. She refused to believe Clayton and her family would not try to rescue her. In the meantime, she had to gather what information she could to help herself and Ellie. Sitting around waiting for people to rescue you didn't work too well.

"Ellie, we need to gather information. I have a friend I can tell what we found out. It might help him find us. We are in the basement with a dirt floor, meaning the house is very old. It might be considered abandoned. Could have the windows boarded up or the door padlocked. We know the man makes sauerkraut. He also possibly has access to veterinarian drugs. You've seen him."

Ellie interrupted her. "How will you tell your friend?"

Um, that was a hard one to explain. "We have a telepathic connection. He knows I've been kidnapped. He's trying to get help now."

Ellie considered her statement for a second. "Is he a witch, too?"

That was a good question. One her mother would have asked if she'd ever had a chance to meet the man. "I'm not sure, but we're very close, have been for years."

Ellie voice sounded a little exasperated, which was a nice change from hopeless. "How can you be close and not…"

The sound of tires on gravel stopped her questioning. Ellie hissed as if he could hear from the outside. "He's back. Get back to your cot. He won't be pleased that you've been moving around."

The rasping of a lock sounded. Padlock, not a regular door lock. The sound of chains falling confirmed this. The exterior door groaned a protest as he opened it.

Great Goddess, help me now. Nora shuffle-walked as fast as she could, creating a cloud of dust in the process. She was about a foot from the cot when she tripped, falling onto the mattress. Now, all she had to do was flip over and get her legs up. Nothing could be done about the blindfold.

A masculine voice joyfully called out, "Honey, I'm home."

She squeezed her eyes shut. The familiar voice touched her, chilled her. People thought the evil you didn't know was bad. Those people had never really known anyone thoroughly evil. Unfortunately, she had.

The basement door swung open.

Chapter Fourteen

The footsteps reverberated as her captor worked his way down the stairs. His pace was slow, as if he deliberately prolonged her agony, but maybe the man was simply tired, too. Exhaustion might work in her favor. He might be too weary to torture her or Ellie or carry out whatever his plans were. It took all of her concentration to keep her breath even as if she were sleeping. Why hadn't she used the time to come up with a plan as opposed to waddling all over the place like a penguin?

Wait, the footsteps had stopped, on the stairs at least. The dirt floor wouldn't make any sound. The swish of stiff fabric rubbing together came closer.

Keep eyes shut lightly, not squeezed shut, body relaxed, not tense, and perfectly still. She reminded herself of what the surgery patients looked like when they were fully under the anesthesia. Maybe she could fool him and buy herself a little bit more time. She didn't know for what, since no foolproof escape techniques took form. All she knew was she refused to be a victim. Realizing her captor probably expected to take her against her will, similar to Ellie, she gritted her teeth.

A tsking sound erupted from the man beside her. "You almost had me fooled, Nora. Until your jaw jutted out and your nostrils flared with anger. Even though I saw signs you'd been busy in the paths in the dirt and your discarded blindfold." He tsked again.

Did it serve any purpose to keep her eyes closed? It was better to be prepared. If she drew her legs up, she could still manage a good push or kick. Her eyes flickered open, confirming what she already knew. It was the jerk from the diner, the one who always wanted to talk to her about his meal. Bonnie fussing over him had never been enough. He'd always wanted Nora's attention.

His dark eyes glistened with delight as he observed her bound state. His smell was rank, fetid, as if someone or something had died inside of him.

His hand came closer, allowing her to see the dirt under his fingernails. Nasty. She'd never noticed him being so filthy at the diner. Her eyes drifted down to his pants, which appeared to be new and stiff, though the knees were dirty, as if he'd been kneeling in dirt.

The man wasn't dressed as a laborer. His appearance made her think of an accountant or some middle manager who would always find fault with his under-lings' performance. His physique was on the soft side, not a man who earned his pay with his muscles.

Her eyes drifted back to his knees. The dirt meant something. *Think.*

He laughed. He pointed at her with one index finger. "I see where your eyes are. I chose you for your cooking abilities. My previous cook is no more." He attempted to look sorrowful, but he failed when he turned his eyes to the floor, especially when he'd spoken with laughter still in his tone.

My previous cook is no more.

She seriously doubted anyone would voluntarily cook for him. Maybe the man had a profile on some dating site. Unfortunately, there might be one or two women desperate enough to cook for him. Not too many, though, she assumed, since he always seemed to be at the diner.

Distraction was her plan. The police would be on their way if she were in a crime drama. "Far as I can tell, you ate at the diner five days out of seven." Her voice came out raspy but controlled. Good.

"Your throat is dry. I'll have to fix that. Gotta take care of my investment. Took me awhile to find a cook I liked. Yours wasn't the only diner I visited." He grinned, showing all of his teeth, even a gray incisor.

That tooth was dead, Nora noted. Lifeless, like his soul. The man was without even intrinsic values. No use appealing to his compassion or logic. He had neither.

Where was everyone? Shouldn't Tonya have raised a search party by now? Where was Clayton? Something touched her. It was more like a feeling that she wasn't alone. There weren't any voices in her head, besides her own screaming in panic.

Prolong the conversation. "Um, how did you pick me?"

He squatted and placed a grimy hand on her hair, stroking as if she were a cat. Ellie whimpered in the distance.

Nora kept her eyes locked with his, watching him as if he were a deadly cobra that would strike the instant, she broke visual contact. Her breaths were shallow as she tried not to suck in the awful odor. Part of her mind worked on the smell, trying to pinpoint it. Another part pleaded with any spirits, any entities to assist her.

Lord and Lady, forgive me for not honoring you properly.

"Nora," the man crooned, inching even closer. "You may call me Neal. Neal and Nora." He chanted the names in a singsong fashion. "We were meant to be together. That's what I thought the first time you came out of the kitchen when I complained about your cooking."

"There was nothing wrong with the burger. You admitted it when I came out. Why me?" What had she done to make him choose her over anyone else? Not that she would have wanted anyone to replace her.

Her eyes drifted to his bushy, unkempt eyebrows. She couldn't keep looking into his eyes. Nana had often commented that she could see evil or feel it roll off a person. How she did used to puzzle Nora. Seeing evil wasn't particularly hard when looking into Neal's bloodshot eyes. His pupils were small, which shouldn't be too surprising in the dim light, but they were more narrow, rather like a snake's. How could she have not noticed that before?

All the times he'd insisted on seeing her she'd usually looked beside his head as opposed to into his face. His accusations that she hadn't cooked something right had made her angry enough that she'd deliberately looked away from the man. Barb would have been all over her if she'd glared at a customer. Chances were, she wouldn't have been here if she'd told Neal what he could do to himself. Of course, she'd have been out of a job, too. Unemployed would have been infinitely preferable to her current state.

Neal kept stroking her hair as he spoke, his grimy fingers sometimes touching her cheek. "I'm a meat and potatoes kind of guy. I chose the smaller diners. No way I could snatch someone out of a bustling kitchen." He chuckled as if he'd found her question amusing.

Nora had turned down jobs at bigger establishments because they wouldn't give her enough hours. Order Up was the only one to provide free meals and guarantee her enough hours to pay her rent. It had seemed like the only logical choice at the time. Part of her mind turned over various scenarios. If the police didn't find her, would her face end up on flyers? Nana would insist on doing memorial ceremonies, maybe even monthly.

Neal continued to talk. It was fortunate he enjoyed explaining his twisted rationale. Nora was willing to bet few people listened to him any other time.

"I found most places tend to hire men as cooks. I had no use for some cranky old man who chain-smoked as he cooked. Definitely didn't want that muscle-bound guy who works the shift after you. Nope, I wanted a woman. Hard to find one in the small diners. I found another woman, but she looked to me the type to win in a knife fight. She overcooked the eggs, too."

Her history professor used to say no good deed goes unpunished. Nora used to think it was a dark way of looking at things. Apparently, giving too much attention to her cooking hadn't paid off.

What could she ask him next?

"I decided on you because you could cook the way I like my food. You were always polite, even though it almost killed you sometimes. It made me think you'd be an easy one to train. The fact you've already trotted all over the room and ripped off your blindfold shows I've underestimated you."

Her breathing stopped for a second as she held her breath. He was on to her, but what captive didn't try to escape? As long as he remained confident in his superiority, he'd slip up. It was time for her critical thinking skills to kick in. A memory nudged at her. Her parents had allowed her to join a scout troop.

At first, they'd been reluctant, fearing the troop might support traditional religious views, but their first activity had found approval. Her first scout excursion had been her last, though. Their troop had planned to help clean up the shore of the local river. Images of her young self proudly wearing her uniform, skipping along the shore with another girl, brought back the joy she'd had at the start of the trip. Truthfully, Amber and she had done very little trash pickup. Instead, they'd played hide-and-seek in the small caves that riddled the shore. One of the parent chaperones had complained it wasn't a great place to be after discovering the homeless took refuge in the caves. The leader must have decided that was a good enough reason to gather up the girls, at the same time that Amber had screamed.

Nora had gone to locate her new friend, only to find her pointing at a shallow grotto from which a stench had emanated, wrapping its horrendous scent tendrils around them. Somehow, Nora had known enough not to look in the cave. Later on, she'd heard her parents whispering about the dead body Amber had found.

Her body went rigid on its own. Dead body. He *smelled* like a dead body. He'd mentioned the former cook was "no more." Ellie had said she'd thought there might have been someone upstairs. Sweet Goddess, would she ever see the light of day again?

Neal quit stroking her head. "What's wrong?" He looked at her quizzically, as if confused why there might be something wrong with being captive. "Oh, oh, I got it." He pulled a large knife out of his pocket. A reddish-brown substance covered most of the blade. "I know what you want."

Nora recognized immediately that it was dried blood, even without the familiar coppery scent. Most likely, the blood belonged to the former cook. She wondered what the cook had done to merit death. Burn the eggs?

Shrinking away from him was the best she could do as he lowered the knife. Kick. She needed to kick with her legs. Partially drawing them up, she was almost ready when he threw his body weight onto her, pinning her legs against the mattress.

"What's wrong with you?" He grunted as he kept her legs firmly held in place. "I was trying to cut the rope off so you could go to the bathroom and cook me dinner."

Cut the rope off her feet. "Nothing. I will need the rope off my hands to cook. What ingredients have you brought me?"

Neal sawed away at her ankle restraints while she considered what she needed to do. A meal rich in starch, bread, and sugar would make him sluggish. It might also give her the tools she needed to make her escape. Did the man have any spices? Remnants of the ropes fell to the floor. A sensation of pins and needles started in her feet. Neal pulled her into a sitting position then helped her up.

The last thing Nora wanted was to lean on her possible murderer, but even with the ropes off, her stiff legs were uncooperative. She was able to shuffle, but bending her knees to ascend the stairs hurt. Swallowing her pain, she limped up the stairs with Neal's help. Her chances of escape would improve greatly if she were above ground. Her thoughts drifted back to Ellie as she gained the first floor. She couldn't leave Ellie behind even if she had the opportunity to escape. The girl had to go with her.

Neal shepherded her down a narrow hallway. Empty squares on the wall indicated pictures had once hung there. The peeling floral wallpaper and the dusty floor confirmed Nora's initial suspicion that the structure was derelict.

A rank sewage odor came from an open doorway. It looked like they'd arrived. Nora remembered Ellie's description of what had happened in the bathroom. Instead of entering, she held her hands out. "I need my hands free."

Neal shook his head. "I'll help you with your pants."

Nora stared him down. No way were things going to go down as he planned. "If you make the mistake of helping me and think to help yourself, then there will not be food."

His head came up fast, and he fixed a bewildered look on her. "No food? None? You won't cook?"

The man actually looked uncertain. A former soldier had mentioned in her psych class that it was hard to deal with terrorists because they were always willing to die for their cause. A person who had no fear of death could not be threatened. War used the threat of death to coerce people into doing things. She decided to make her point more clear.

"None." If her hands had been free, she'd have crossed her arms. She leaned against the wall, hoping she appeared stronger than she felt. With any luck, her leaning would look like nonchalance.

The knife reappeared in Neal's hand. The blade came closer to Nora's face, allowing her to see the serrated edge. "What if I threaten to kill you? You'd cook for me then."

Her eyes followed the knife as he waved it in front of her face.

Show no fear. Bluff.

She wasn't sure if it was her thought or possibly Clayton's. It still sounded like good advice.

"Go ahead and kill me. You'd just have to start the hunt for a cook again. In the meantime, I guess you'd be cooking your own dinner." Despite her bonds, she managed to shrug her shoulders, pretending she could care less if he plunged the knife in her heart. Her loose cook whites covered her quivering legs.

Neal stared at her for a few more seconds, cursed, and then lowered the knife to the rope at her wrists. "I thought you would be easy to boss around. If I knew you'd be this difficult, I would have kept looking."

Her bonds off, she darted into the bathroom and slammed the door shut before Neal could squeeze in. With the door shut, one foot and shoulder wedged against it to keep it closed, she felt for the lock, found the knob and twisted, not that it would do that much good. A butter knife could spring the locks on the interior doors except for Ellie's padlocked one. Neal already had a knife.

The absolute darkness made the smell worse. Her fingers flipped the light switch, but nothing happened. "What's wrong with the light?" she grumbled, mainly to herself.

"Burnt out two months ago," Neal said. "No reason to replace it since I always leave the door open."

Not something Nora wanted to contemplate. Moving her right foot slowly forward, she found the toilet. Squatting in the general direction of the commode, she hurriedly peed. Neal could come through the door at any time. She pulled up her adult diaper, actually glad of it. She was unwilling to touch anything in the filthy place to blindly search for toilet paper. A shiver passed through her before she yanked the door open. Might as well discover what she had at her disposal in the kitchen.

A smart cook could disable a threat with the food she served. Neal would not provide her with any handy poisons, but if she had the right herbs, she could make him very uncomfortable. A man retching his guts up tended to make mistakes.

Neal stood right outside the door, startling Nora for a second. Did he have a clue what she was thinking?

He grabbed her arm, dragging her behind him into a cluttered kitchen. A rickety fridge, which appeared fifty years out of date, had a red cooler sitting in front of it. An equally ancient stove served as a base for a camp stove with a flexible hose attached it to a propane tank. *Propane.* There was potential. Make that, potential for killing the three of them if she wasn't careful.

"Where's the food and pans?" She mentally cataloged everything in the cluttered room, sorting it all into two divisions: things that might help her to escape and things that wouldn't. Newspapers, dirty dishes, a scrapbook, and a pair of scissors covered a rectangular Formica table. The scrapbook and papers indicated Neal was keeping track of his crimes. That demonstrated a certain amount of pride and egotism, which meant she might be able to flatter him. Most people didn't have an inflated sense of self-worth, which was why they downplayed flattery and tended to be suspicious of people who were in actual awe of them.

Neal pointed with the knife toward a drawer underneath the oven. "In there."

Turning to keep him in view, she squatted to reach the drawer. She wouldn't put it past him to stab her in the back. Logically, that would put him out of a meal, but she doubted logic actually played a part in his thought processes. If it had, he wouldn't be grabbing women off the streets or out of diners.

Her fingers wrapped around a heavy cast iron skillet. One whack with the skillet should knock her captor out cold, maybe giving her enough time to rescue Ellie. She eased the heavy skillet out of the drawer and turned slightly, using her body to block her weapon, and straightened slowly. Her only window of opportunity was to catch him unaware.

Normalcy was the key as if she cooked for her kidnapper every day. "So, I notice you're using propane when you have electricity."

"Electricity has been shut off to this house for years. I got the lights on a gas generator. Running the stove and fridge would take too much fuel. No heat or air, either, not that there was all that much when I lived here as a kid."

A clue. *He used to live in this abandoned house, away from everyone else. Good chance the title is in his name.* She felt as if she'd shouted the words in her mind, but there was no hint Clayton had heard them. What did she expect him to do? Best he could do was to write a letter in his time addressed to Adam and Maura Carpenter. What were the chances it would find its way across the centuries into the right hands in a prompt fashion?

Not knowing how to answer Neal's previous statement, she ignored it. Instead, she asked about dinner, hoping to get him to drop his guard. "What did you say you brought for me to cook?" Her head pivoted with her question while both hands kept a firm grip on the skillet.

"I didn't say." The man met her glance with eyes filled with silent laughter, probably due to the pistol in his hand pointed straight at her back.

Damn. Pistol beats a skillet every time. Where had that come from? She hadn't noticed it earlier.

Neal answered her silent question. "It's obvious to me that you are much smarter than the others. They could be controlled by their fears and some force. Never even had to display the Sig to get them to do what I wanted. You're a different matter. More difficult, more cunning. You'll be more of a challenge to break, but I will break you." His lips tilted up to match the laughter in his eyes.

Think again. I am the sharper knife in this drawer.

No way would she give him the satisfaction of seeing her distress. Nora turned back to the stove, staring at the skillet with food stuck to it. "Is there any way to clean this? It's disgusting."

His voice caused her to jump, since it was closer than she'd expected. "Water in the sink. It's all cold from the well, but I guess you could scrub on the pan."

Neal was only a foot behind her. He must have moved closer while she'd tried to concoct an escape plan. The gun barrel rubbed against her neck.

"Nora, Nora, what you need is a man to take charge of you. I am the man to do it."

His fetid breath brushed the back of her neck. The thought of his dirt-encrusted fingers on her body caused vomit to creep up her throat. A gulp sent it back. If there were no escape for her, then she'd prefer to die now. If she could get him to shoot the propane tank, they'd all go up in a fiery death. It wasn't the ending she'd pictured for herself, but she'd not be his sex slave.

Should she elbow him first or lead with the skillet? There was a chance he might shoot her no matter what, which would be preferable to dying in a fire. If she failed, then another captured woman would take her place. Apparently, Ellie had failed in the cooking capacity. "I could start on dinner as soon as you give me the supplies." Her goal was to have her voice sound normal, as if she were discussing the possibility of rain.

The pistol barrel dropped away from her neck as he took a step back. She heard the sound of paper rustling as he pushed a grocery bag toward her with his foot. The man wasn't taking any chances. What had she done to indicate she'd be a challenge? Too bad, she couldn't go back and rethink that strategy. A bag of potatoes crowded the bag, along with a tube of hamburger, onions, and burger buns. She'd be making his favorite diner meal, with some modifications.

The ingredients didn't yield much hope as far as a means to escape, though a heavy meal of fried potatoes and burger should render him lethargic. The potato bag smacked the scarred counter as she dropped it, sending up a small cloud of dust. The place was filthy.

Currently, she had to appease Neal if only for the fact he was holding a gun on her. He'd want a diner-quality meal prepared on a camp stove, a test she never would have asked for. At one time, she'd thought having the love of her life in another century was trial enough. Speaking of that, where was Clayton?

I'm here. I tried to come to you, but all I managed to do was float around the room like a ghost.

That explained the feeling she'd had in the basement.

I'm not sure why I can't cross over. Nora, darling, this frustrates me more than I can tell. Stall. As much as it pains me to say it, play to his vanity. Insist you want to make a meal worthy of him. Ask for spices.

Spices. She'd already thought of that but hadn't asked for them. Still, she had to try. "Do you have any condiments? Cayenne pepper, ginger, garlic?" She tried to remember which spices would cause the runs in high doses. Listing unusual spices might make him suspicious, though. "And salt. Do you have any cooking oil? I'll need it to fry the potatoes."

Neal shoved some items around behind her. He slammed a box of table salt, followed by one of black pepper. "That's all I got. Don't see why you need all those other spices."

Well, that wouldn't do her much good. She unpacked the rest of the items from the bag. *Oh, I need those spices to cause stomach cramps and keep you in the bathroom for the majority of the night.* Nora chose not to share her thoughts. "I want to make dinner special for you." Luckily, she wasn't facing him, which allowed her grimace to go unnoticed. "I want to make you a dinner you deserve." Did she ever.

Neal grunted in response. "Sounds good. Not tonight. I'll try to pick those up tomorrow. Anything else you need to get started on the food tonight?"

She glanced at the supplies assembled on the counter. Her eyes lingered on the onions, nature's laxative. Of course, combined with red meat, bread, and potatoes, she might end up making the man regular. Geesh. Why couldn't she wear a poison ring like a Borgia? A flick of poison, while it wouldn't be enough to kill him, it would be sufficient to have him writhing in pain while she and Ellie escaped.

"I need a cutting board, plate, paper towels, spatula, and a knife." She listed the requests in a practical tone, unsure of how he might react.

"Knife? You think I am stupid enough to give you a sharp knife?" Neal half-growled the words as if to make a point.

It would be easy to answer his rhetorical question, but a bullet would be her most likely reward. Instead, she opened the potato bag. Nora pulled out a couple of potatoes and placed them in the skillet. She added a few onions, too. Turning, she brandished the skillet in front of Neal, who still held the gun on her. "I suppose we can try cooking the potatoes like this. Guaranteed to be burnt on one side and raw on the other. The other option is cutting them into home fries, which will reduce your wait."

His eyes flickered over the skillet, before he withdrew the bloodstained hunting knife from his pocket and offered it hilt first. "Remember, I'll have my gun on you every minute. Bullets are faster than a knife."

He held out the knife for several seconds, drawing her eyes like a magnet. No doubt, the blood on the knife was from the last failed cook. No way could she bring herself to even touch it. The knife could serve as evidence connecting Neal to the missing woman. "Um, do you have anything smaller? I might cut myself peeling the potatoes."

Neal pocketed the knife before stooping to blindly root through a cabinet as he kept his eyes and gun trained on Nora. He pulled a rusty steak knife out and offered it.

Nora's hand closed over the blade. Her thumb rested on the blade, feeling its dull edge. Peeling anything with this knife would be difficult. Best she'd go with just slicing the potatoes. "What about the cutting board?"

Neal slapped the table with his free hand. The noise startled her, making her jump, much to her captor's amusement. "I don't have any damn cutting board. Where do you think you are, the diner?" He chuckled at his own perceived wit.

The scarred counter probably held enough germs to wipe out an army, which wasn't exactly a bad thing, though heat tended to kill most germs. Even if Neal did contract some bug from ingesting the various microbes in the house, it wouldn't be fast acting.

The dull knife made cutting the potatoes difficult. The knowledge that a lunatic with a gun stood less than a yard away made it worse.

Act calm.

The words felt like something she might say, but they weren't hers. Nor were they Clayton's.

Help is on the way.

That had to be wishful thinking. She wanted to believe someone would rush in to save her.

A small pile of potato slices formed on one side of the counter. Soon, she'd switch to onions, which would make her eyes water. Too bad, she couldn't get Neal to chop, but she could keep him busy.

"How do you turn this stove on? I need the cooking oil if you want your potatoes to be crispy as opposed to sticking to the skillet and crumbled."

She had her hand on the last potato and her eyes lowered as she watched Neal root about the kitchen through her lashes. He swore as he pawed through the cabinets. She thought about rushing him when he was halfway into the cabinet, but the man could easily shoot through the cheap cabinets. What she needed was some way to disable him.

Knife was dull. No available spices for stomach cramps, and any viral infections would work too slowly. Neal pulled out a dusty tin of oil that appeared ancient.

He held the oil aloft. "I found some. Might be a little old, but oil never goes bad."

"Good." She pushed the word out, stopping herself from explaining that oil does go rancid. That's why she kept hers in the fridge.

He placed the dusty can beside the potatoes. A quick glance confirmed that the can itself would probably bring a few bucks from itinerant antique and junk dealers. A plan formed in her mind. "I need the stove on, too."

A quick twist loosened the lid. A whiff of the heavy, foul aroma indicated it had gone bad. Still good for her purposes, she decided, as she began to pour a generous quantity into the skillet.

Neal watched her as he fiddled with the propane tank. He awkwardly clutched the gun, as he pushed the lighter mechanism on the camp stove. A huge flame appeared along with the rotten-egg smell of propone. Neal almost fell backward as the flame leaped up, but he caught his balance then adjusted the flame.

Talk about missed opportunity, Nora grumbled to herself. Still, she had a plan.

The cast iron skillet smoked a little as it heated, demonstrating she must have splashed some liquid on the exterior of the pan. She sliced onions into the skillet. Even Neal would be suspicious if all she did was heat the oil. Silently, she beseeched the elements for help.

Fire, assist me in my endeavor. Air, carry my pleas for help to those who can understand your language. Earth, give me strength to do what I must do.

A simple sideways step brought her into a half-turned position. Neal's hand still gripped the pistol, but his interest was on the newspaper. He flipped the pages. "I'll be able to paste your missing story soon."

No article for your scrapbook, you mean. Instead, she replied, "Paper doesn't get too excited about college kids. They are always disappearing. Usually turns out they went home, went to another college to visit friends, or even took off with their current squeeze."

She threw a potato slice in the grease and watched it sizzle slightly. Not hot enough. The combined fumes of the propane and rancid oil made it hard to breathe. Did Neal notice the smell? If so, she needed to distract him to keep him from investigating. It wouldn't do for him to discover she was heating oil as opposed to frying potatoes.

She slid to stand in front of the stove, blocking his view of the skillet and the bubbling oil. Hot pads would be nice, but she didn't dare ask for any. Her damp hands rubbed down her loose white top. If it had been bigger, she might have been able to use it as a hot pad, but she wanted the pan away from her body when she tossed the hot oil on Neal. Her best bet was to go for his face. How much would the oil incapacitate him? On television, the people usually fell to the floor, screaming in pain, leaving the good people plenty of time to escape. Nora knew better than to take what she saw on television as accurate.

The camp stove made a slight hiss while the oil bubbled. Her captor hummed the theme song of a television show she couldn't name. Underneath it all, she thought she heard something, maybe a stick breaking or bush rustling.

A quick glance at Neal revealed no alarm over the possibility of someone snooping closer to his house. Maybe she'd imagined the noise.

Hold on, Nora, we're coming.

The voice again. Not Clayton's. It was her grandfather. She was sure of it. How could she not recognize her own grandfather? Could be the kidnapping and drugging had slowed her down.

The sound of a dog barking close by jerked Neal out of his perusal of the newspaper. He sprang out of the chair and rushed to the boarded-up window.

On his tiptoes, he tried to peer out between the slats. "I think someone is out there. It is hard to tell with the falling light. It could be just kids and a dog. After all, I've used this house for over two years, and no one ever bothered to come looking."

Nora knew the time had come to act.

CHAPTER FIFTEEN

Goddess, give me strength.

She glanced at Neal's back, willing him to turn. It would do her little good to hit him in the back. He held the gun loosely in his hand as he peered out the window.

"Can't see anyone. Must be a stray dog." Neal started to turn. "When are those hamburgers going to be ready?"

Grabbing hold of the hot skillet handle with both hands, she bit her lip as her hands burned and tightened against the blistering heat. Hot oil splattered her hands as she tried to hold the skillet level.

"Right about now." She launched the hot oil in Neal's direction. The oil spattered him as if in slow motion, covering his face, shirt, and arms. Burn blisters formed immediately. The gun dropped from his hand, and he fell to the floor with anguished screams.

She lobbed the skillet at him. It bounced off him, causing him to yelp. "Bitch, you'll pay."

The man wasn't as incapacitated as she would have liked, so she didn't have much time to release Ellie and get out of there. She scooped up the gun with one hand, tucking it in her waistband at the small of her back. There had to be something she could use to release the girl. As she ran for the stairs, she scoured the area, begging any good spirits to assist her. It was highly doubtful any existed in such a horrible place. An old, weathered hammer caught her eye.

She might be able to pry the door open or at least break off the knob. "Ellie, I'm coming. Try to break the door down from your side."

The sound of a body hitting the door assured her Ellie was trying to help. In her rush, Nora missed a step and rolled down the remaining ones. Dizzy, she stood up, shook her head to clear it, and then went to grab the hammer.

The door looked more formidable up close. The small hammer didn't appear capable of tearing the door from its hinges. How one man managed to get the door down the stairs was short of amazing, unless he'd had help. Not something, she wanted to consider.

The first blow with the hammer reverberated all the way up her arm. Steel, it was a steel door. No way would she be able to take that down.

Running would be her best bet. She'd bring back help. "Ellie, I am going to have to get help."

"Don't leave me. I'll die here." The pleas dissolved into weeping.

Hammer in hand, Nora looked between the door and the steps. She couldn't leave Ellie. What if Neal killed the girl while Nora tried to find her way back to civilization? He would burn the whole place down to hide the evidence. The thought of Ellie trapped inside like a caged animal caused her to examine the box-like cell.

The hammer hit the plywood vigorously, knocking a small hole in the board. A big-enough hole would allow Ellie to crawl out.

Crouching at the end of a square of plywood, she found a place where the two boards came together. It was a tiny space, but enough room to edge the claw end of the hammer into the crack. She pulled back with all her weight. A three-foot section splintered off, sending her windmilling backward before crashing against the sauerkraut wooden trays with a thud spilling fermenting cabbage on her and the floor.

Ellie's voice urged her back up. "I think I can see some light. Hurry, please. There's another panel inside. You can break it."

Nora pushed the sauerkraut off her face. The salty liquid on her hands exacerbated the pain from the burns. *Goddess, help me now.*

Hammer in hand, she crawled to the small opening she'd made and felt for the interior wall. The low-hanging plywood made it hard to get much force behind her hammer pounds, but on the first hit, the board crumpled, which caused Ellie to squeal from the other side.

Together, they knocked and pulled at the drywall to create a space big enough for Ellie to crawl through. Excited at the idea of escaping, both women worked feverishly, throwing drywall pieces to the side. The only noise that filled the small area was their labored breathing and the soft falls of drywall chunks. *Almost done. They would escape.*

A knife tip touched her throat, stilling Nora's actions. A slight twist of the knife left a long slash on her neck. Blood flowed down her neck as Neal hauled her up by the waistband of her pants. The medical professional in her automatically diagnosed the cut as a surface wound that wouldn't kill her. The blood would probably congeal in a couple of minutes. No doubt, the man intended to make her pay.

Grabbing for the gun, she was horrified to discover it was no longer in her waistband. She must have lost it in her tumble down the stairs. Neal tried to haul her upright but stumbled, dropping her. Nora rolled to get out of reach, resorting to techniques she'd learned in her self-defense class.

No needle full of animal tranquilizer would take her down this time. Her movement brought her up under the stairs. No gun in any obvious location. It must have fallen under something. She needed a weapon—anything.

Neal regained his balance and headed her way, half his face blistered with third-degree burns and one eye swollen shut. A grim, determined set to his lips promised retribution, but his footsteps were unsteady, showing some signs of trauma.

A weapon, any weapon, might be enough to bring him down. Like a hammer. It was next to the wall. Somehow, she had to get close enough to pick it up without signaling her intentions. She sidled closer to the wall, keeping eye contact. The last thing she needed was for Neil to look down. "Not as fast as you used to be, old man."

Neal growled in response but kept walking toward her. "I underestimated you. I won't do that again. Obviously, you have more brains than that silly fireworks slut."

Nora moved her body to the right, though she planned to go left, sure Neal would go right to attempt to grab her. A quick glance to her left revealed a filthy blonde in a bikini top and shorts, kneeling by the hole she'd so recently crawled out from. Ellie held the hammer in both hands.

Time to think of another weapon. Better yet, it was time to move Neal closer to Ellie who had the hammer. Most likely, Ellie would crumple when confronted with her attacker. At least, that is what most pop psychology believed.

What would be a good weapon? The gun would make a great weapon, but no sign of that. Sauerkraut. The memory of the salty juice stinging her burnt hands inspired her to work her way toward the kraut, moving herself and involuntarily Neal away from the squatting Ellie.

"You can run, but you're not going anywhere. Go ahead and wear yourself down. It will only make it easier for me."

Nora contemplated everything she'd like to say, but she needed to get to the sauerkraut. The open crate beckoned her. She did her best to ignore the pain as she submerged her hands into kraut, grabbing huge handfuls to fling.

Neal walked closer, chuckling to himself. "Is this your big escape plan? To put your hands in sauerkraut? I'll admit I make good kraut, but it won't be your salvation."

In the split second before she flung her string missiles, she considered the man in front of her. People would consider him ordinary, nothing special, too bland to be considered attractive, a trifle wimpy and on the soft side. Most would dismiss him as harmless. Despite her initial impression that he was evil, she'd refused to listen to her instincts. Well, she knew better now.

Ellie straightened from her squatting position. She sidled across the room, never taking her eyes off Neal. Nora cut her eyes toward the steps, signaling her to get help. Neal, catching the eye movement, started to turn. The first sauerkraut launch splattered harmlessly against his shirt.

"Really? You're throwing sauerkraut? Just when I thought you might be smarter than the average woman, you do something that confirms you're not."

The second handful slapped him in the face. "Stupid woman, that hurts." He swiped away dripping strands. Nora pelted him with two more handfuls.

Ellie held her hammer over her head like a Norse Goddess and sprinted for Neal, slamming the tool into his skull. The man dropped to his knees. Ellie pounded about his head and shoulders, driving him to the floor. She screamed as she struck the steel head against his vulnerable body. "This is for ruining my life! Stealing my belief in the basic goodness of people! Causing my mother endless worry! Raping me again and again!"

Nora seized the hammer from her hand. "Ellie, you can't kill him." She tried to herd the hysterical girl up the stairs.

The girl shook off her shepherding arm. "I can kill him. I need to."

She made a grab for the bloody hammer that Nora held out of reach. The slender girl clawed at Nora in her frenzied state, opening up the burn blisters on her hands. Only a firm belief in harming none kept the hammer clutched in her hand.

"Ellie, he has to stay alive so he can be punished. Besides, he knows where the bodies are."

Ellie's hands dropped to her sides. "Bodies." She said the word as if it were a foreign language she didn't comprehend.

The sound of breaking wood sounding from the rooms above cut short Nora's explanation about possible other abductees. Ellie grabbed her arm, tears welling in her eyes. "What now?"

A strong masculine voice shouted as footsteps ran across the room. "Police!"

A familiar female voice cut through the sound of running feet and shouts of "Clear!" coming from the various rooms. "I know my granddaughter is here."

"Ma'am, you have to wait outside," a man answered.

Ellie whispered as if afraid of being overhead. "Is that your grandmother?"

Before Nora could answer, Nana's voice sounded closer to the basement door. "Get out of my way, officer, before I turn you into a toad. I can do it, too."

A police officer stood in the doorway with Nana peering around him to yell, "That's my granddaughter and fellow victim, Ellie!" She poked the policeman. "You might discover she's a missing person you failed to find."

Sometimes her grandmother could be opinionated enough to find herself inside a jail cell. The woman continued to try to get around the officer blocking her. "Ma'am, this is a crime scene. You'll contaminate it."

Nana pointed into a corner of the basement. "Look, my husband and Clayton are already downstairs."

Nora turned slowly, not expecting to see Clayton. Not really expecting her grandfather, either. Clayton jogged across the basement, sidestepping the unconscious kidnapper.

He held his arms wide. "Nora, my darling, I came for ya."

The policeman jogged down the stairs. "How did you two get in? I told you to wait outside."

Her grandfather made a bow in the officer's direction. "I've mastered teleportation. We couldn't wait. I thought we would give the girls a hand, but it looks like they managed on their own." He nodded in the direction of the prone man. "That man smells evil."

Ellie, perhaps feeling more normal now that the danger had passed, quipped, "That's sauerkraut."

Clayton herded Nora and Ellie toward the stairs, Nana and Grandfather following. Nora stopped near the confused officer. "Don't let him die without finding out where he buried the other woman."

Ellie repeated the words in the sudden silence. "Other woman?"

They stepped outside into a heavily wooded area. Nora twisted to look back at the house. The windows were boarded up, except for one that allowed a triangle of light to spill out. The paint was peeling on the neglected building showing plain weathered wood. Those who passed by the house would consider it abandoned. Then again, she doubted many came so far out from the main road.

A policewoman met them, speaking into her shoulder-mounted walkie-talkie. The uniformed woman used her flashlight to guide them through the dark woods to where a small fleet of police cars, an ambulance, and even a SWAT van waited. A K-9 officer kept a short leash on a large dog. Had he and the dog tracked them, and if so, how? Nora was sure she'd arrived in a van, even if she didn't remember the details.

It was almost full dark, especially with the sheltering trees. The vehicles' headlights illuminated the scene, giving it a surreal feeling as groups of officers huddled together. The crisp air with a hint of winter in it was a welcome change from the foul-smelling house.

Nora gave the girl beside her a quick glance. Ellie had arrived in the summer and was leaving in the cool fall weather. A male paramedic shook out a blanket to place around Ellie, but the girl shied away from him. Intercepting the man, Nora took the blanket and wrapped it around the shivering girl. It would be a long time before Ellie would be able to look at an unfamiliar man without fear.

Clayton stayed behind Nora as she headed for the rest of her family huddled behind the police line where two officers kept watch over the small group. The officers directed suspicious stares at Clayton and her grandparents. Nana's complaints carried in the still air.

"If the stubborn police would have believed me when I told them that Clayton had astral-projected to the area, we would have been here so much sooner. Ignorant fools."

Her outspoken grandmother's grumbling brought an upward twitch to Nora's lips. *At least some things stayed the same in her very topsy-turvy world.*

She startled when Clayton placed a hand on her lower back, a very solid, real-feeling hand.

How had he gotten here? Would he stay or blink back in time once she no longer needed him? Turning, she grabbed Clayton's hand, intertwined her fingers with his, and squeezed hard. "I can't believe you're here. In case you're wondering, I need you all the time—as in forever."

Clayton used their clasped hands to pull her closer. "At last, you've finally figured out we were meant to be together."

She half-whispered, "Yes," but knew he heard.

Tonya waited with Nora's parents and siblings, Ethan and Leah. Clayton let go of her long enough for everyone to hug her. It felt good to be alive and so well loved.

Ellie stood at the edge of the group wrapped in the blanket. Maura, Nora's mother, handed her a cell phone. "I am not sure how cell service is out here, but if we all work together, I think we can give it a little boost."

The small group circled Ellie. She held the phone up to her ear, and her countenance wavered between uncertain and outright fear, until someone picked up on the other end.

"Mom, it's me. I'm alive."

The tears flowed down the young woman's face as she assured her mother she'd see her soon. As she sobbed harder, Maura took the phone and spoke into it.

"Hello, I'm Maura. My daughter Nora was a kidnap victim, too… Yes, I know you want to be here. I know how you feel. If it hadn't been for the determination of my daughter's"—she glanced at Clayton—"boyfriend, I doubt we would have found the two of them. The man searched day and night with no more than a few leads after she vanished from her workplace."

That answered a few of Nora's questions.

Leaving the warm embrace of Clayton's arms, she walked over to Ellie and hugged her, rocking her slightly. Remembering the trauma she'd felt after her own rape, she made sure to tell Ellie what she wished someone had told her all those years ago. "It's okay. It's over. It's in the past. It's not your fault. There are evil people in the world who do evil things. You were simply in the path of one evil person, that's all."

Ellie quit sobbing enough to look up with reddened eyes. "People will know. People will judge me. I'm dirty."

The words were familiar. The same as what she'd thought herself. Tightening her embrace, she reassured Ellie. "No reason for people to know. Your name won't be in the paper."

"It has to be. It's news."

"It is. I agree. I am okay with reading Nora Carpenter and another woman were rescued." She pushed the dirty blond hair out of Ellie's eyes.

Ellie looked up in disbelief. "You can do that, how?"

How indeed? It had never amazed her for a moment to see her family standing outside the house. That's who they were. No matter what, they supported one another. Strange to think she hadn't told them about her rape. They wouldn't have judged her. Somehow, they had known and never mentioned it, just doing what they knew would help her. Their sudden move, her grandmother's insistence on giving her cleansing potions and protections spells, her mother taking her to the Y for self-defense classes, all indicated some knowledge. She'd chosen not to tell because she'd blamed herself. At the time, she'd thought she'd somehow brought shame on the Wiccan community. At the time, she'd rationalized that her behavior and Abby's, as proud Wiccans, had invited the violence.

Now, she realized that the two of them had only been females in the wrong place at the wrong time. It was important that Ellie realized this about herself, too. Together, they'd shared a struggle against unthinkable evil that most people wouldn't understand. Leaning toward the other girl, Nora touched her head to Ellie's. It was then that she vowed to always be there for Ellie.

"You've met my family. They are a force to be reckoned with. News media don't reveal the identities of rape victims. You'll be okay. You might want to finish out the school year at home, or at least until you feel like returning to school."

Using her hand to wipe her nose, the girl nodded. "Yeah, that sounds good right now." She looked around at the circle of people surrounding her. "Your family is pretty cool."

A man followed by another man carrying a large video camera on his shoulder attempted to film her and Ellie. It only took a glance in the direction of the cameraman, and he fell, dropping the camera. The sound of the camera hitting the ground and shattering into several parts, along with the reporter's cursing, assured Nora that there would be no live interviews tonight.

Three probable culprits—Nana, her grandfather and Clayton—all sported identical grins. No wonder the man had fallen so hard.

The cameraman stood, brushing the dirt from his clothes. His glance swept the ground suspiciously. "There's nothing there. Not a tree root or a rock. It felt like my feet were pulled out from under me."

Nora patted her friend's shoulder. "See? I told you it would all work out."

A burst of pride swelled up inside her. It was an emotion she hadn't experienced in a while. She'd always considered her family decent people. Somehow, being pagan in a non-pagan world made them more special and precious. They were the salmon swimming upstream in a world of religious conformity.

Leaves crackled under Tonya's feet as she headed their way. She angled her head in Clayton's direction. "So that's your honey? I can see why you might trip through time to find him."

Ellie looked up inquiringly, but Tonya didn't notice the girl's look of astonishment as she continued, "Even in those old-timey clothes, he's still sexy. Never have I witnessed a man who loves a woman as much as he does you. Your grandfather searched until he found a portal and was able to connect with him. Clayton came through to get to our time. Even knowing he could never go back, he never hesitated."

Nora met Clayton's eyes. "Of course he didn't hesitate. That's the way it is with soul mates. You just know."

Tonya directed a small push at Nora's shoulder. "Listen to you, sounding so sure of yourself. A couple of days ago, you weren't."

Her roommate was right. Amazing how looming death made all the pieces fall into place. "A few days ago, I was worried about graduating. That pales in comparison when you consider dying and your method of death. I'm thankful, very thankful, to be alive and to have another opportunity to love my soul mate over there." She winked at Clayton, drawing a laugh from him.

The reporter edged closer, asking the waiting officers for information. Most ignored him, while a few offered, "No comment."

The diligent reporter had turned in the direction of the small group when a large barn owl took aim at his head, causing him to drop to the ground.

A few officers took delicious delight in the reporter being the one harassed as opposed to the other way around.

Her grandmother's distinctive voice carried over the noise of the man hitting the ground and the laughter. "Buell, I did not cause that owl to dive at that annoying news fellow. That was natural. Don't underestimate nature."

Nora watched her grandparents good-naturedly bicker. She knew as well as her grandfather did that the owl was Nana's creature. Owls were her token animal. It could have carried a banner reading, "This owl attacked you courtesy of Esmeralda Hare."

Noise near the front of the house caused Ellie to huddle closer to Nora. She wrapped one arm around the girl, pulling her closer. Together, they watched two SWAT officers wrestle a handcuffed Neal down the porch stairs. Despite the large, armed men on either side of him, he kept up a constant stream of profanity, debasing the female gender. His head jerked to where Nora and Ellie stood. He managed to stop long enough to direct a glare so malevolent at the two that it seemed to glow in the evening air.

Clayton moved in front of Nora and Ellie, blocking Neal's view of them with his strong body. "Be glad," he growled, "that the police are taking you away. If I had my way, you would pay a thousand times over for the evil you did. You'd not live long enough to see the inside of a cell."

Nora could see only the masculine back blocking out all the evilness pouring off her kidnapper. She felt safer, warmer, with Clayton protecting her from harm. His voice became deeper as he made his final pronouncement. "I may not be able to touch you. Rest assured, though, consequences will occur in this lifetime and in all your future lifetimes."

Neal's cursing shut off as the police car door slammed on his tirade. The waiting personnel turned toward the huddled group while a few drifted off to the house to photograph and map out the crime scene.

A female medic motioned to Nora. "Ma'am, we need the two of you to go to the hospital and be checked out."

Ellie snuggled closer to Nora. Sensing her fear, Nora offered an alternative suggestion. "Couldn't we just drive to the hospital in a car? I think there has been enough trauma in Ellie's life. Her mother could meet us there."

The medic's eyes roamed over the two of them. "Not really standard procedure. I could get in trouble if you don't arrive via ambulance." The woman glanced back at the other medics waiting beside the ambulance, clearly torn about what to do.

Nora's mother, Maura, worked her way to the front of the group. She touched the medic's arm. "I'm a registered nurse with the trauma unit at St. George's. I can monitor their condition as we drive to the hospital. I have to agree with my daughter. Anything else might be too much at this point."

The medic ran a hand through her short, bleached locks. "Well, um, this is highly unusual." Her gaze went back to the other medic and driver who had drifted over to chat with the remaining officers.

One of the officer said, "Barton, let them go in their own cars. We'll give them a police escort to the hospital. Probably better all the way around."

The medic gave a short nod. She pivoted and walked back to the ambulance. Nora watched the stiffness in the woman's shoulders; sorry for her annoyance, but if it helped Ellie even a little, then they could deal with breaking protocol.

The officer who'd sent the unhappy medic on her way turned to face the group. "I guess we'll all head out to St. George's. I'll lead the way. You can follow me. We'll debrief you once we get there. Grieg"—he pointed to the other officer—"will follow you."

Nana grumbled under her breath about procedures

The shadow of a large owl blocked the moon as it cruised over their heads. "Esme," Nora's grandfather hissed, "behave. We have to get these girls to the hospital. Later on, you can rant. Why you never saw the inside of a holding cell baffles me."

"Who says I haven't? You don't know everything, Buell."

Her grandmother kissed Nora on the forehead, and her weathered hand rested on Ellie's cheek. "Be at peace, child. The worst is over."

Ellie's stiff body relaxed in Nora's arms. Nora kept one arm hooked around her waist just to keep her upright. Her mother joined her, wrapping an arm around Ellie's other side. The two of them half-walked and partially dragged her to the sedan.

Her father directed car assignments. "Leah, Tonya, Ethan, go with the Nana and Grandpa. Clayton, you ride shotgun with me."

The cars crept down the dirt road in a ragtag line until they hit the paved road, where their escorts turned on the sirens and lights, clearing the way but never going above fifty. They probably doubted her grandparents could keep up.

The lights and buildings flashed by Nora's window. It was almost like another world, one she'd left not so long ago.

It must be even odder for Ellie, who had lost months of her life. Nora's arm stayed wrapped around her new friend. The now-sleeping girl's head rested against her shoulder. Nana had a knack for putting people at ease.

The sleeping girl resurrected memories of Abby. There had to be something Nora could do for Abby. It was time for Abby to break out of her self-imposed shell. Nora possessed the hammer to help break through her calcified exterior.

The hospital passed in a whirl of stainless steel counters, white-coated individuals, and an antiseptic odor as they were hustled through emergency as priority patients with an entourage that included uniformed officers. People probably thought they were criminals of some sort. A weary-looking blond woman sprang up at their entrance.

Her gait and direction sent her on a collision course for Ellie. A policeman stepped in front of her, blocking her. Her head popped around the officer's body.

"That's my baby, Ellie." Her voice carried as they were rushed through swinging doors. "That's my baby. I have to see her. I thought she was dead."

The door swung back into place. Ellie stayed glued to Nora's side, whispering. "I can't see her. What do I say? I'm not the girl who left for work so many weeks ago. As the door shut, she whispered to herself, "Might as well be dead."

Nora gave the whispering female a squeeze. "I heard that. I know how you feel, but believe it or not, you can get past this, too. Make up a story if you want. I used to worry about all the people in my high school knowing. Ironically, only months later I cut ties with all of them. That's how little they mattered in my life."

Ellie shivered, wrapping her blanket tighter. "Easy for you to say. You're strong. You have a family that cares about you."

Nora inhaled deeply. How could she make Ellie understand? Putting both her hands on Ellie's shoulders, she turned her, making them eye to eye. "First, I don't ever want to hear you say you're not strong. You survived. That makes you very strong. People who love you will always love you. This doesn't affect how they perceive you. Be careful that you do not allow your self-perception to be altered."

Ellie's teeth worried her bottom lip. "I know you're right. Still, I feel so dirty."

Wrapping her arms around her, Nora hugged her hard. "That will pass, too. Trust me."

A nurse attempted to separate them to direct Ellie into a room for an examination. Ellie's grip on Nora tightened. No way should Ellie experience a medical exam with strangers probing her body and discussing her as if she weren't in the room. It was another reason why many rape victims hesitated to report the crime.

Nora looked at the nurse's name badge. "Nurse Cooper, I think you can understand that Ellie has been through a great deal. The examination, while required, is not only uncomfortable, but also emotionally trying. I want to be in the room with her."

The nurse nodded, flashed an understanding smile and handed her a cloth gown. "See if you can get your friend into this."

Nora accepted the gown with one arm still wrapped around Ellie. Nora turned to ask her mother to inform Ellie's mom to get clothes for her, but all her family was gone, including Clayton. Her gaze swiveled around the small room, expecting them to appear. The nurse, noticing her distress, answered her unspoken question.

"They aren't allowed back here until after you've been processed."

Ellie mumbled, "Processed—whatever that means." She shrugged her thin shoulders.

Of course, Nora knew that. She'd worked in hospitals enough to know that. They were outside the door somewhere, milling around with all the other anxious loved ones. "I should have remembered. I guess I expected—no, never mind."

She searched her mind for Clayton, finding nothing but her own thoughts. Did that mean with him here in this century with her they could no longer share thoughts? They'd have to communicate the way other people do with all their garbled messages and things not said. "I can't believe it."

Ellie nodded in agreement. "Your grandmother wasn't one to give up easily. I thought my mother was loud, but your grandmother was telling him how it was and waving her cane. They might have even called security if it wasn't for your grandfather."

Strange, Nora hadn't noticed any of that. Ellie's abuse and thoughts of Abby consumed her. She'd often wondered what she'd end up doing with her degree, and now she knew. Her purpose was to help rape victims.

Shaking out the gown, she held it out to Ellie. "You need to put this on. They'll take your clothes for evidence. I'm sure you don't ever want to see them again anyway."

Ellie took the gown and turned to undress, talking all the while. "You got that right. I doubt I'll ever wear a pair of shorts or bikini top again."

Nora wanted to tell her she would, but she hadn't herself. She'd avoided all clothes that were even vaguely feminine, convinced that the smallest ruffle or display of skin would turn men into beasts. The nurse picked up the discarded clothing with latex gloved hands and bagged it.

A female doctor handled the examination, putting Ellie at ease. The doctor also solidified Nora's desire to work at a rape-crisis center or even in an emergency room. Brutalized women did not do well with men examining them, even one with medical intentions.

Ellie held on to Nora's hand all through the exam. The doctor didn't talk too much. The few comments she made were about how brave and clever they'd been to escape the maniac. Nora was about ready to explain that the police had rescued them after following Clayton's tip, but she didn't.

A mental replay of a burned Neal hopping down the steps unrolled, along with the fight that had followed, rubbing salt into his burns via the sauerkraut, and the hammer to the head. The man had been down and out. The two of them could have run out of the house. They'd have been in the middle of who knows where, but she had confidence they'd have found a way to civilization. Together, they'd conquered their fears enough to fight back. *Concentrate on the solution, not the problem,* was her grandfather's advice. It had worked for them.

Chapter Sixteen

Ellie's father stood in the lobby, looking both lost and weary. His clothes were rumpled, his hair mussed, not a bit like the debonair charmer Nora had expected from his daughter's description. The only way she knew it was him was the way his face lit up when Ellie walked through the ER doors dressed in blue scrubs the nurse had found for her.

Nora touched her friend's hand, passing her the scrap of paper on which she'd scribbled her phone number. Her intention was to stay in touch, but she wouldn't be surprised if Ellie chose not to. After all, Nora represented a very bad experience in her life. She would want to forget everything associated with that time. If that were the case, Nora would understand.

The hospital had allowed only the mothers in after the initial examination, while a parade of relatives crowded the already busy waiting area. Nana probably had already worn out her welcome with her previous behavior. Nora's family stood as she exited with her mother. She watched as Ellie ran to her father's arms. Tears rolled down the man's face, not the actions of a man who abandoned his daughter along with his former wife.

Her own family stood with expectant faces, reminding her of when Leah and Granddad had returned from the past only a few years ago. Speaking of the past, where was Clayton?

As if hearing his name, he came around the corner. Spotting her, he broke into a jog to get to her, where he wrapped his arms around her and swung her around.

The admitting nurse stood and shook a finger in their direction. "None of that." The twinkle in her eye revealed her true feelings, despite her words. Laughing, Clayton put her down. Turning to the nurse, he placed one hand over his heart.

"Forgive me, ma'am. The sight of my beloved overwhelmed me. To spare you from the joy of our reunion, we'll depart."

The nine of them crowded out the door, practically emptying the waiting room. A brief parking lot consultation had them all heading to the pancake house for something to eat. Nora attempted to demur explaining she must look and smell horrible, but her family pushed aside her worries.

Her brother Ethan wrinkled up his nose as if sniffing. "Not too bad, I've smelled plenty worse."

A quick spray of perfume, a comb through her short hair and the hoodie sweatshirt Leah handed her made her ready to eat breakfast closer to midnight.

Over pumpkin pancakes and sausage, Tonya revealed how she'd discovered Nora was missing. "It was probably eleven when I realized you weren't home. It didn't seem right. I called the diner. Brandon answered the phone and told me you'd stomped off in a tizzy. I explained to him that you had no way to get home but the bus, and the buses stopped running at ten."

Clayton speared the last bite of his pancake and gestured with the syrup-laden morsel. "This Brandon is no friend of yours. He doesn't care enough to make sure you get on the bus safely."

Nora felt obligated to protest but reconsidered. Brandon had made sure other nights. Mentioning how thoughtful Brandon could be might only rile Clayton. Ogden, on the other hand, was a jerk who wouldn't have made the effort to make sure she was safe. Still, if Brandon and Ogden had noticed her absence earlier, the police search could have started much sooner. Clayton had jumped centuries without a second thought.

"Did Brandon say anything after that?" Nora asked.

Tonya shook her head. "I did get a call back from a waitress."

Nora gestured at her to continue. "What did she say?"

The server hovered nearby, refilling coffee cups. After she stepped away from the table, Tonya continued, "She walked in when Brandon and Ogden were arguing, attracting the attention of most of the people in the diner. Bonnie was leaning on the counter watching, too. The waitress saw this creepy guy get up to go to the restroom. Said something about waiting for him to come out because she didn't want to meet up with him in the narrow hallway. Turns out that he never "came back. "

"Did no one else notice?" It seemed like it should have been such a no-brainer.

Grandfather felt the need to comment. "People seldom notice what is right in front of them."

Nana and her father agreed. Tonya looked at the three, grumbling about unobservant people. "The waitress who worked the next shift, I forgot her name, mentioned it to both Brandon and Bonnie. The man left his money on the table for the food, which meant Bonnie didn't care too much, how he left. They did find your backpack still in the kitchen with your bus pass, wallet, house keys, and phone. They knew then you hadn't left on your own."

Clayton wrapped his arm around Nora, pulling her closer under the disapproving eyes of both her father and grandfather. Her father cleared his throat, but her sweetie left his arm where it was and asked, "What took so long to locate this evil man?"

Her mother joined the conversation. "The police called him a person of interest. They didn't know he took Nora. No one knew his name or where he lived. Even if he had given out any information, it could all have been false, considering he'd planned ahead of time to take Nora."

The memory of the elderly couple warning her and taking her home came to mind. "Oh, oh, there was a couple who runs the metaphysical book shop in the south end, the one with past-life readings and aura photographs."

Nana's brow wrinkled for a moment before she announced, "Martha and Owen Carlisle."

"That's right." Nora had forgotten their names but remembered they knew her grandmother. "I was going to have some past-life readings done so I could better understand how Clayton and I were connected."

Clayton's lips touched her hair, causing her brother to exclaim, "Please, some of us are still eating."

Instead of Ethan's behavior offending him, Clayton laughed. "Become accustomed to it."

Her brother grinned, but continued eating to the point of reaching for Leah's sausage. She slapped his hand, but then placed the link on her brother's plate.

"Anyhow," Nora said, trying to gather her thoughts. "They wanted to tell me something bad was headed my way. They drove me home because they didn't want me to take the bus. The two sweet dears acted like they worked for a secret government agency as they drove through the streets as if we were being followed."

Grandfather quipped between sips of coffee, "They were probably being followed, not you."

That seemed odd, but she chose not to reply to it. "All they wanted was for me to be safe. Martha kept saying something about how she had to protect the granddaughter of Esmeralda Hare."

Nana slammed her cane on the floor for emphasis. "Damn right. Now, why didn't they protect you?"

"They tried. Owen checked the apartment. The couple even did a protection spell on every window and door. Of course, I left and went to work. It was my day off, too. The new guy they hired never works. He's always calling in. Come to think of it, it's odd Neal was there that night at all. He usually wasn't when I don't work." Nora took a sip of water, turning the idea over in her head.

Leah looked up from eating. "Who's Neal?"

"The kidnapper." Nora picked up a bacon strip and chewed on it. It was rubbery and fatty. Obviously, the cook did not understand the concept of crisp bacon. "Doug, as a cook, is useless. It didn't seem like the man wanted to work.

He'd been around for weeks occasionally working but usually not. The fact he wasn't fired bears witness to how hard it is to get someone to work swing shift."

Her father directed his gaze at her. "Explain. I can see the wheels turning. Share your thoughts."

"Well, I hate to accuse an innocent man. No one can figure out why Doug even works at the diner. He is always coming up with excuses why he can't. Once or twice might be believable, but not all the time. I had to work that night because he called in with an excuse. From what my co-workers said, Neal came in only on the days I worked, apparently the better to harass me. Everyone noticed it, too. I'd call that night a coincidence, except Neal had had a syringe full of ketamine, what had to have been chloroform, and his van parked outside of the diner's back door. Sounds premeditated to me."

A white business card rested on her father's plate as he punched out the number on his phone. "Detective, remember you said I should give you a call if we thought of something."

Clayton whispered in her ear. "Your family is the vengeful type. Makes a person pay for hurting one of their own. Whatever happened to your attackers?"

Nora looked down at her plate. "I try not to think about them. A friend told me they lost every game that season, but that hardly seems enough. I guess the few who were counting on scholarships lost them."

His hand tightened on hers as he half-whispered, "Tell me their names, I'll hunt them down. No one hurts you without retribution. I don't care if it was in the past."

Before she could answer, Nana rapped his legs with her cane. "I like your spirit. As for the boys, none of them came to a good end. One is in prison due to a sexual-battery charge."

Nora snorted, not surprised. She wanted to ask whom, but was unsure if she could even attach the names to faces anymore.

Holding up one finger as if remembering, Nana continued, "Another one was murdered, not sure who did the killing or the why behind it. I have my suspicions, though."

Clayton squeezed Nora's hand before murmuring, "Sounds like I'm not the only person seeking revenge."

Leah interrupted. "I remember that case. They ruled it was self-defense, even though the circumstances were suspicious."

Nora nodded at her grandmother to continue. If anyone would know, Nana would. She had more contacts than the FBI with both living and dead informants.

The waitress hovered as she poured coffee, her eyes growing large. Unashamed of her eavesdropping, she added, "Are you talking about the cursed football players? Saw a special on television the other night, one of those news magazine things."

Grandfather raised both eyebrows as he inquired, "What did the program say?"

Putting the coffeepot down, the waitress raised both hands to gesture as she talked. "Local football team starters were bound for big college scholarships. Rumor was they were bullies. Beat up the nerdy boys and assaulted their share of girls, too. The only problem was people tended not to believe the girls because the football players were golden boys with rich parents."

Seeing everyone's attention was on her, the server smiled and continued. She looked behind her to see if anyone was watching from the kitchen before she leaned forward to convey the rest of her story. "One of the former students from the school called the football team cursed. At some point, they assaulted the wrong person, or people. Everything went wrong for them. Losing games, they should have won. One died in a motorcycle accident. Another one, driving drunk, is now paralyzed. You were talking about the others. None of them came out okay. That's why people say they were cursed."

The waitress reached for her coffeepot and gave an emphatic nod. "I figure they got what was coming to them. You can't do that much evil and not expect some consequences."

Her father slapped the table. "Amen to that, sister."

His unexpected comment and action caused the family to erupt into laughter, except for Nora. Had she caused all the misfortune that had happened to her attackers? Did that make her an evil person?

Clayton's half-hearted laughter stilled as he noticed her silence. Placing his head next to her bent head, he whispered, "Never blame yourself. Evil sows its own consequences. We both know the fates will have their way."

Her teeth worried her bottom lip. She'd like to believe Clayton. It would certainly resolve some of her guilt. "You don't understand. I cursed them."

His fingers untangled from hers. Did he find her repugnant now? No. Using both hands, Clayton framed her face and gently pulled it up for her to look into his caring eyes. "Let me ask you this, Nora, my love. Did you fight your attackers?"

Why was he asking her that? He had to know she'd fought. "Yes. I did." She forced the words out through gritted teeth. This is why she'd chosen not to go to the police. She was afraid of questions like this. "I kicked, screamed, and bit, but there were so many of them. They laughed at my efforts."

Tears blurred her vision. As she blinked to hold them back, Clayton's thumbs wiped away those that escaped. "Now, sweet darling, I do not want to make you cry. All I wanted for you to see was that your curses were only a way of fighting back. As for them harming those monsters, I imagine many have cursed them long and hard. Together, all the curses and strong emotions may have hastened their consequences, which is as it should be."

Nana raised her cane over the table to nudge at Clayton's shoulder. "Are you making my granddaughter cry? Keep in mind, we are not the forgiving sort. Very vengeful. Break Nora's heart and it will do you no good to hide in the past, because I will find you."

Sometimes family could make you want to drop into the floor, no matter how well meaning.

Clayton gave Nora a kiss on the cheek. "Nora is my soul mate, and she has been the last seven lifetimes. Destiny has made it so."

Her Irish charmer faced down her daunting Nana. Her grandfather folded his hands, and his countenance took on a somber expression. "Been riding on destiny all these centuries? Well, it ends here. You have to prove yourself worthy of my granddaughter."

Her family had gone all nineteenth century on her. Clayton didn't seem too disturbed. He stroked his chin before asking, "What would you have me to do to prove myself?"

Her father was the first to answer. "How would you provide for my daughter?"

Great Goddess, she wanted to hide her face. There was no way Clayton could provide for her. He'd come from another time and had no skills to work in this century. That didn't matter to her, though. If all he did was love her that would be enough. Eventually, he could learn new skills, maybe even go into medicine.

Clayton removed his arm and placed both hands on the table. When he spoke, his voice no longer held a trace of laughter. "I've known about Nora longer than she realized. I was waiting for her in the wrong century. Some people assumed that the Irish are shiftless, given to drinking and fighting. I'm not. In fact, I've been blessed by my fey grandmother with the gift of knowing. Sometimes, it is what card to play in a poker game. Other times what stock to invest in. These skills allowed me to acquire wealth that I squirreled away in different places from hiding it in the ground to having a trust made up for a Nora Carpenter not yet born. It is not as unheard of as you might think. People set up trusts all the time for children not born. I also buried a box of gold in your backyard."

Her mother gave him a dubious look. "How did you know where to bury it? How do you know someone hasn't dug it up?"

They were probably the same questions Nora would have asked if she'd had a chance. It would be interesting to hear his answers.

Clayton's familiar smile reappeared. "The plot of land your house sits on has stayed in the same family. My family, actually, after I bought the property, buried my treasure, and asked my cousin to watch over it. Not the same house, but pretty much in the same location."

Nora's mouth dropped open. Who was this wheeler-dealer from times gone by? Where had her gentle healer gone?

Clayton reached for her hand and entangled their fingers. "Did you truly think I managed on the occasional chicken or firewood a grateful family gave me?"

His question caught her unawares, because she'd thought just that. "Well, yes, I did. I would have loved you as a simple traveling healer. I did love you."

He brought her hand up to his lips for a kiss. "Do you not love me anymore, then?"

Aware of all the interested stares and listening ears, she decided to demur. Why announce her feelings in front of everyone? "We haven't even had a real date yet." Thinking of an older word he'd understand, she added, "You haven't courted me."

Still holding her hand, his eyes twinkled as he looked into hers. "If it's a courtship you're wanting, I promise you a grand one. But I hope not to use up all my gold wooing you, especially when you had a women's crisis clinic in mind."

"How did you know?" Here she'd thought he couldn't read her mind in present time. Apparently, he was as heavy-handed about it when they were both in the same time.

Clayton winked, causing Nana to hoot. "Reminds me of you, Buell, back when you were young and handsome."

Everyone at the table laughed at Nana's remark, except for Grandfather. He looked affronted. Holding a hand to his chest, he asked, "I'm still handsome, right?"

Each one of them rushed to assure him he was the most handsome ceremonial magician they knew, which catered to his vanity. He settled back into his seat with a contented expression.

Nora's mother elbowed her father. "I am going to enjoy watching this courtship."

Tonya chimed in from the other end of the table. "I know I am, especially from the girl who was not going to have anything to do with men."

Clayton sat up, quickly to correct. "She is still not going to have anything to do with men, just me."

They all chuckled, as intended. Nora looked around at her family, including Clayton and Tonya. The things she'd worried about amazed her when only family truly mattered. Well, and love, of course, and her health.

Her grandfather's face registered a measure of chagrin as he sat ramrod straight. "I am the only ceremonial magician you know."

Then there was humor, too. She could live well on love and laughter. Very well.

EPILOGUE

It was hard to believe it had been a year since she and Ellie had first met. An electronic buzz alerted her that Ellie had arrived. "She's here."

Clayton, checking off supplies on his clipboard, stopped and looked up with a grin. "I'll stay here and allow the two of you your reunion."

"You're the best." She kissed her handsome husband's cheek before dashing down the hallway like a giddy six-year-old instead of behaving like a sedate director of a sexual-trauma clinic and rehab center.

Security at the clinic was tight. Not just anyone made it past the lobby doors. Traumatized women didn't need people trooping around making a difficult situation worse.

A confident, smiling Ellie waited, along with her father, in the cozy lobby crowded with overstuffed furniture and live plants. A large aquarium full of colorful fish took up most of the area next to the reception desk. Ellie turned to the worried-looking man. "See? Nora's here, I'm fine. Come back in a couple of hours."

Ellie's father looked unsure, but then started for the door. His hand rested on the door as he turned to look at Nora. "Keep her safe."

The petite blonde woman rolled her eyes. "He's like that all the time. I swear, my mother is worse. No way I'm going away to college, either."

Nora hugged the still-talking woman. "I will," she assured the father as he exited. Addressing her friend, she added, "Of course, they worry about you. They feel responsible even if they aren't. They're acting out of guilt. You seem to be dealing with everything fairly well."

"I'm okay." She grimaced a little. "I didn't really want to go away to college. I prefer to stay home, but I don't want my parents to know that. It would probably make them even more overprotective."

Nora nodded, totally understanding. "I'm glad you came. Your continual contribution to our group for recovering from rape is a big help, especially today."

"Why today?" Ellie's eyebrows lifted with curiosity.

Nora motioned to the left corridor and turned in that direction as she spoke. "Remember my friend, Abby?"

"Yes." Ellie lengthened the word as Nora pushed open an unfamiliar door.

A young woman reading a book looked up at their entrance and smiled. "I see you brought me company."

"Ellie, I'd like you to meet my best friend, Abby."

The suddenly silent Ellie looked from Nora to Abby, then back again. Thrusting out her hand to the seated Abby, she said, "I'm thrilled to meet you. Better yet, talk to you."

Abby took the outstretched hand. "Me, too. It's been awhile since I could actually communicate with my visitors. Thanks to my parents' devotion and Nora's concentrated efforts, I found my way home." She sighed deeply and released Ellie's hand. "For a long time, I was wandering around in some mental fog. This one"—she gestured to Nora—"she's been saving the world and conducting an across-the-centuries romance while I slept."

Nora tucked a hank of Abby's hair behind her ear. "That I did. I was waiting for your assistance with the women's center. I'll need your help, too, Ellie."

Abby stood up, swaying slightly as if she wasn't used to standing. "I'm here now. I believe this calls for a group hug." The three of them wrapped their arms around each other, laughing, and crying, too. That continued the healing for all of them.

Love, acceptance, and finding your purpose comprised the best medicine of all.

THE END

If you've enjoyed this book, a review would help others and make the author's day too.

You also might appreciate the first book in the Pagan Eyes series, Initiation.

http://www.amazon.com/Pagan-Eyes-Initiation-Rayna-Noire-ebook/dp/B00HKKYRF2/ref=sr_1_1?s=digital-text&ie=UTF8&qid=1394413946&sr=1-1&keywords=pagan+eyes+initiation

The third book in the series, Declaration, the brother's tale, is coming in late June 2014.

Find out more at the website: *www.raynanoire.weebly.com* or the author page *www.facebook.com/AuthorRaynaNoire.*

Follow at: *www.twitter.com/raynanoire*